THE SPECTATORS

Kano Press

Also by Betsy Robinson

Cats on a Pole

Plan Z by Leslie Kove

The Last Will & Testament of Zelda McFigg

Girl Stories & Game Plays

*Conversations with Mom: An Aging Baby Boomer,
in Need of an Elder, Writes to Her Dead Mother*

THE SPECTATORS

by Betsy Robinson

In Saint Stylites, the famous Christian hermit of old times,
who built him a lofty stone pillar in the desert and spent
the whole latter portion of his life on its summit, hoisting
his food from the ground with a tackle; in him we have a
remarkable instance of a dauntless stander-of-mast-heads;
who was not to be driven from his place by fogs or frosts,
rain, hail, or sleet; but valiantly facing everything out to the
last, literally died at his post.

—HERMAN MELVILLE, *Moby Dick*

. . . right now, I am comforted by imagining what the world
looks like from the height of a soaring hawk, as the sun
sweeps over the green hills, the glistening rivers, the empty
streets, pushing back the night, as it has done, and as it will
do, until the end of time.

—KATHLEEN DEAN MOORE, *Earth's Wild Music:
Celebrating and Defending the Songs of the Natural World*

"Don't judge me," he said.
"Ain't," the kid said.
"What is it you're doin' then?"
"Just watchin' is all."
"Watching what?"
The kid stood up and pitched the stick into the fire. "Guess
I'll tell you when I got that figured. Right now, I'm just
watching."

—RICHARD WAGAMESE, *Medicine Walk*

The navel is a scar on people's abdomen, which formed
when the remains of the umbilical cord dropped off. When
a child is born, the umbilical cord is clamped and then cut
to sever the link between mother and child. The first scar is
therefore connected to the mother.

—AUÐUR AVA ÓLAFSDÓTTIR, *Hotel Silence*
(trans. Brian FitzGibbon)

CHAPTER 1

I came late. I was not there at the start of the event. Yet I can envision the details as though I were. It is a Monday in early January of 2017. A partly sunny afternoon in New York City. Thirty-seven degrees. High humidity, maybe a drizzle on the way. The view up Broadway is overcast. The two relatively new high-rises on either side of West Seventy-second Street are muted in the fog, ugly against the gray sky, and the old-world, tiered wedding-cake beauty of the Ansonia Hotel just north on Seventy-fourth almost apologizes for them. A small flock of gray pigeons soars in counterclockwise circles from the east side of Amsterdam Avenue over the CapitalOne Bank, climbing in altitude west over the land-marked Central Savings building, spreading and diving southwest, then compacting into a tight clump of silver slivers as the sun hits their bodies through a brief break in the clouds over the islands of Verdi Square and the Seventy-second Street IRT subway station. Morning rush hour is long over and it will be more than an hour till the streets clog with neighborhood residents pouring out of the station in exhausted yet impatient herds. The traffic light at the fork where Broadway splits into upper Broadway and Amsterdam is yellow when the white van with the "Trump for President" sticker rear-ends the bug-like Smartcar, throwing it onto its side as the van's driver careens left, through the guardrail and into the subway station. Some freeze, others dive; bodies fly, bones crack. A horrible accident! A man in a hardhat working on a scaffold above the Tasty Café on Seventy-first vaults to the street and runs to help. Women scream. Babies shriek. What a crazy driver! Call 9-1-1! yells the hardhat. People on cell phones turn them to record as bodies are dragged out from under the van. *The driver. Check the driver!*

A wide-bodied, middle-aged Black woman in a cheap wool coat over violet scrubs hurtles a fragile White woman in a wheelchair across the street away from the accident and parks her next to the benches on Verdi Square. "I've heard these benches have bedbugs," says the White woman haughtily, eying a crow perched on the bench back; odd that he didn't fly off at the crash.

"Wait for me," answers the Black woman, and then she waddles as fast as her weight will allow back across the street, and that's when the van blows up.

Lily Hogue, the discomfited woman in the wheelchair, tracks the upsurge and scattering of pigeons at the sound of an explosion as the van bursts into flame. She forgot her eyeglasses in the restaurant, but if she tries very hard, if she squints so tightly that her sea-blue eyes tear, as if viewing in her mind's eye a play being played through a scrim by the tiny people fleeing the scene, if she breathes low into her sagging belly, she can remember as clearly as I see this day that she was once a member of the scurry. Although she was born with her mother's thick, flaxen hair, good bone structure, and, eventually, the long, leggy gams of a super model, now her hair is so wispy and white that, when sunlit, it's merely translucent fluff, exposing Lily as a pink-scalped head atop a bone-thin face with crinkled paper-like skin; she has not aged well due to the recent stress. But considering the alternative, the fact that she *has* aged certainly is a coup. Lily is a month shy of sixty-six—old for a family where everybody died young—wars, suicides, accidents, three killed at one time by falling off a mountaintop, several murders, and at least one electrocution by lightning. Her longevity is due to good luck and the fact that she has not been particularly adventuresome. Until today.

Her attendant is clearly dead. Lily knows this from the sound and the heat that is radiating from the other side of the street. She supposes that getting back to the restaurant to retrieve her eyeglasses is no longer an option. She wonders if Medicare will pay for a second eye exam in one year. There must be a record of the prescription somewhere, but for the life of her, she can't remember where, and Nanette, her attendant, took care of those things.

People are rushing across Amsterdam Avenue to the island of Verdi Square to gawk. As the south end of the square fills, Lily, panting and pushing, laboriously edges her chair toward the north end, far enough from the action not to be singed by the heat, but close enough to feel the air burst when the second explosion comes and the crow finally takes off.

At the blast, she is overwhelmed by déjà vu and painfully aware that this is no accident, and she remembers all that is to follow.

There are never any accidents. I know that now that I have watched this whole story play out. Only cycles and patterns—patterns of movement, patterns of events, patterns of attractions and aversions. Right now, for instance, in the present scene, there is an avid throng of onlookers at the south end of the square. Some are crying, others are trying to push to the front, certain that they can help or at least be part of the action because they are People Who Act. In front of them, in the street, several police officers who appeared out of who-knows-where are bellowing orders. Sirens wail from south on Amsterdam where the fire station has stopped traffic and dispatched every truck on the premises. As the crowd balloons, they expand toward the north end of the square. There is a group of teenagers screaming and laughing hysterically, not because they are amused, but because they must release their explosive adolescent energy, their response to the tragedy. Near the front are two girls, maybe fifteen, and Lily feels a familiarity as she watches their dance: One is sparkly-eyed and sure of herself as she points, directing her friend to take a photo of her and to make certain she gets a good angle so it's clear that sparkle-eyes is part of what will no doubt be a historic act of terrorism on the six o'clock news. Maybe they can even get their video on TV. The girl with the cell phone camera wears a pale yellow parka with a fur-fringed hood. "Cathy, now!" yells sparkle-eyes. "What's the matter with you?" Sparkle-eyes has perfectly symmetrical features, a sharp little nose, and short brown hair curled back to expose gold hoop earrings. "Cathy!"

But Cathy is frozen. Useless.

PART I

The Early Years

Over the course of embryonic and fetal development, as cells evolve to take on the specific characteristics of the hundreds of types of adult tissues, cells are constantly making choices about what kind of cell they will become.

—DANA-FARBER CANCER INSTITUTE

CHAPTER 2

Who knows when it began? The dread, the anxiety, the overwhelm. For Lily, it was first noticed at bath time. Whenever her mother attempted to scrub her tummy, newborn Lily would spasm and flail, erupting in a prolonged, terrified, agonized high-pitched shriek, as though she were being stabbed, until finally in frustration, her mother scrubbed so hard she ripped Lily's umbilical stump and then for weeks probed the mess with a medicated Q-tip to keep it from getting infected, marveling at how much easier it was now that Lily had stopped crying and instead went limp, almost dead.

In the third grade, her teachers noticed the isolation: "Lily Hogue daydreams and does not listen or play well with others," said the fountain-penned note, etched with such force that the impression of the words was visible on the reverse side of the heavy-stock report card.

Lily was born in 1951 into a loud, silently desperate, and enraged family of two athletic and relentlessly competitive brothers and, the year after her birth, an equally energetic sister. Although there were four little Hogues, in temperament and demeanor, Lily was the middle child—quiet and reluctant to join the barely repressed hostility.

The Hogue house was cold—impossible to heat due to shoddy construction, never questioned by Mr. and Mrs. Hogue, who were people of ordinary American tastes: cookouts on the Fourth of July, Sears Roebuck-ordered clothes once a year when the catalog was passed from parents to children with pages marked in red crayon or blue pencil. Mr. Hogue swallowed his resentment at having to commute daily to his job in the city. Mrs. Hogue grocery shopped, cleaned, cooked, and tried her best to keep her nervous breakdowns to herself.

Mr. Hogue was a violent man. Although he never hit his wife or children, his green eyes shone with an ever-present threat. He was tall, dark-haired, much taller than Mrs. Hogue, and stood with the erect posture of a general, which he may or may not have been, since he never spoke about his military service, and everyone, including Mrs. Hogue, knew never to broach the subject. He liked his dinner served on time, his shirt collars starched, but only the collars, and his shoes so shiny he could see his reflection. It was Bob, the eldest son's job to shine Mr. Hogue's shoes and he did so with religious fervor so as not to evoke the ferocity. Mr. Hogue had a glorious smile that conveyed charm and humor and successfully obscured the true nature of his explosive energy.

Mrs. Hogue was once a beautiful woman with limpid blue eyes, such flaxen hair that her eyebrows were invisible, and fine hands. But in marriage, she had a developed the bowed posture of a servant with raw, red hands that perpetually smelled of Lemon Pledge, and her delicacy was obscured by her dedicated devotion to pleasing and avoiding confrontation.

The two eldest sons resembled their father both in appearance and sense of entitlement. The youngest daughter, too, felt the entitlement which made her a target for her brothers who assumed all girls should be like their mother.

Lily quickly developed the talent of being a ghost—so ethereal and quiet that she was nearly invisible. When Mr. Hogue's energy would ripple, portending an eruption, she would silently disappear—to her room, to the woods, to walks around her neighborhood where nobody ever saw her.

One winter day, when the energy in the house felt explosive, she slipped outside with her aluminum flying saucer sled and walked through snowy silence all the way to the golf course, a good two miles, the last leg of which required trespassing through somebody's driveway and out their backyard. But Lily's invisibility made her fearless. There was a group of children on the far hill—the best unobstructed slope for sledding—but Lily trekked alone to the top of the first hill, dappled with rocks and tree remnants, that marked the furthest border of the course. At the peak, she put her eyeglasses in her pocket, took a moment to enjoy the steady *wrrr* of the icy wind blotting out all other sounds, blindly plopped onto her flying saucer, and was off—an eight-year-old's fantasy flight, bitter chill whipping her face, no thought, just speed. Until looming in front of her, dead center and unavoidable in her downward streak, was a blurry tree stump. Of the fight, flight, or freeze responses, Lily chose the latter, eyes frozen open, burned by the icy wind.

"Hold on tight," commanded a warm, maternal voice.

And Lily, who was an obedient child, did. Squeezing shut her eyes to blot out imminent death, she gripped the canvas handholds and suddenly she felt the saucer's front edge tip gently up, followed by a mild skid under her bottom and a bump as she dropped to the ground on the other side of the stump and continued to the base of the hill.

After the ride, Lily stood for a moment, thinking nothing, and then she turned and walked home the way she had come.

She never told anybody about this adventure. She never marveled at the voice. She never thought to wonder why she was spared death or disfigurement or a lifetime in a wheelchair, and yet other children—say a headstrong teenager on a joyride several years later—were not. Perhaps because she was eight and simply accepted what happened as inevitable. Or perhaps, for other reasons.

When Mr. Hogue's energy rippled and quiet disappearance into secret solitary adventures was not an option because there was no obvious getaway route, Lily used an alternate means of escape. She became expert at what was disparagingly labeled by her brothers as the "Lily leap"—a quiet but effective headfirst dive to the floor and quick crawl to safety.

Lily had her mother's fine features, flaxen hair, and no eyebrows, as well as her father's height, so despite her stand-offish nature, she was never bullied. At school, it was assumed she was shy. She was invited to birthday parties and made an appearance in the white dress with red waistband or sash and patent leather Mary Janes that were customary for the era. She was too young to question styles, and she wore what her mother directed. But even then she noticed the patterns—how seemingly overnight a whole town could become obsessed with Hula Hoops or, later, the Beatles. How suddenly every girl in her seventh grade got her ears pierced and inserted with colorful beads and began wearing a boy's name bracelet, signifying that she was going steady. She noticed, but never thought to wonder why she was not a part of these mass movements. She noticed the way you would notice a flock of birds taking off en masse, or a herd of bison stampeding in one of the westerns her father loved, or a world war.

Her brothers and sister loved the westerns also and all things "cowboy," and their father delighted in taking them to the stable at the country club where he boarded his quarter horse—an anomaly in this Westchester enclave of jodhpurs and velvet-covered English hunting caps. On weekends, Mr. Hogue traded what he called his "Buster Brown suit" for blue jeans and Tony Lama cowboy boots. "But Buster Brown wore short pants and a silly scarf," said Mrs. Hogue the first time her husband laughingly described his work uniform, and her husband's piercing green eyes instantly hushed her. Clearly the pejorative was meant to describe Mr. Hogue's feelings about wearing the suit; Mrs. Hogue was wrong and apologized.

"Who's coming with me to the stable?" said Mr. Hogue every Saturday morning. It was understood that the invitation was to the four children, not to Mrs. Hogue. And in the beginning, all four would don their jeans and cowboy boots and pile into the Willie's jeep.

At first contact with a fug of horse musk mixed with the stinging smell of urine and hay, Lily's eyes would water and she'd begin to sneeze. Mr. Hogue and her brothers and sister would push and shove ahead of her into the stable, eager to be first to the stall, because whoever was first got to lead Trouble into the paddock. Trouble had spirit, said Mr. Hogue, proud of the animal's tendency to toss his head, snort, and buck at the first sign of a rider's insecurity. The boys grinned at Lily as she held back, standing at the stable entrance. They grinned even though they didn't look at her. They grinned with their backs. So did Mr. Hogue. Lily's younger sister had not yet picked up the sport of exclusion, but soon would learn that group power comes from keeping others out—namely Mrs. Hogue and Lily. Lily watched how they moved as a group—her father and siblings, clumped on either side of Trouble like human baggage—the way they would move as one, radiating a wall of "get out of our way" to anyone who was not a part of the team. Team spirit, that's what Mr. Hogue liked. With him as the captain.

Trouble had no respect for Lily. At first meeting, he had glanced at her, tossed his mane, and then whacked her out of his way with a swing of his head.

"Lily, get me Trouble's halter," said Mr. Hogue from inside the stall.

Her brothers exchanged a quick, competitive "what gives?" glance.

"I want you to lead Trouble outside today," continued Mr. Hogue as Lily obediently delivered the halter with the lead line attached from the hook outside the stall. "Put it on him."

"Hey!" protested the brothers, but their upset at having their job usurped was quickly quashed by a severe look from their father.

Lily had no desire to take her brothers' job. But she also wanted to obey her father. Maybe she could do this after all. Maybe if she made an effort to participate in what he loved, the gap would dissolve and, even though she seemed allergic to all equine endeavors and didn't enjoy them, maybe she could be a normal member of a family. She thought all this in the two seconds between lifting the halter over Trouble's head and being head-butted and stomped.

"See?" said Bob, as though his point were made. Without a word, Jimmy, the next oldest, grabbed the halter from Lily, easily sliding it over Trouble's head and ears and buckling it on the side.

"I'm sure nothing's broken, but you'd best go check yourself," said Mr. Hogue, annoyed but also satisfied that he'd kept his promise to his wife, who had begged him to include Lily more, and it had proven impractical.

Trembling from humiliation, pain, and a heroic effort to hold back tears, Lily limped away toward the grooms' bathroom. "Meet us at the paddock," called her father. "If you don't feel like riding today, that's fine."

After that, on Saturday mornings when Mr. Hogue would gather the team, he would invite Lily by saying, "Are you sure you won't come?"

"Thanks," Lily would answer, "but I think I'll read today" or "Mother needs my help today."

As soon as her father and siblings were out the door, Mrs. Hogue would retire to her bedroom where she kept an electric space heater and a secret bottle of port, and Lily would go to her room and sit. She would sit and stare, wrapped in a ratty bird blanket that she had attached to as a baby—a musty crocheted thing with a big, black, broken-threaded bird face on it—Lily privately called it "Crow"—that had come down from her mother's side of the family. Mrs. Hogue had kept it by mistake, couldn't even remember why it was in her possession, and had tried to throw it out numerous times, but finally had acceded defeat and allowed Lily to derive whatever comfort she could from it.

And sometimes, wrapped in Crow, Lily would sit and stare and hug herself to music—whatever came on the radio. Oh how she wished she could relive the magic of the music that had once brought the peace. Bach. It was two violins playing Johann Sebastian Bach that changed her, ruining her for anything less than the seven minutes of paradise she briefly knew at age nine. Two violins. They danced, chased, dipped, bowed, inviting each other with tender sweetness. Tenderness as vast as space and sadness, and nothing. Nothing like anything Lily had ever felt. She disappeared in its ocean. No more Lily. Nothing. And to try to preserve this feeling, she began her lifelong habit of keeping a diary: "I felt nothing today." And only she understood that this was a sublime event. Eventually, she did manage to find the music that elicited this bliss, and although she bought every copy she ever came across of *Bach's Concerto for Two Violins and Orchestra in D minor*, never again did she disappear that way.

By senior year, Lily, who had never had a date and had long ago accepted that she would find no numinous sweet nothingness in high school or be a part of mass movement rituals such as prom, was stunned when a new boy named Philip—a nice-looking tall fellow with yellow hair and crooked teeth—called on the telephone and popped the question.

"Are you there, Lily?" he asked, more puzzled than nervous.

"Yes, Philip," she finally gasped. "Yes, I'm here and I'd be happy to go to the prom with you. I shall buy a dress."

A little taken aback but mostly charmed by Lily's practical response, Philip replied, "That's good, I suppose. Okay then."

When Lily agreed to marry Philip four months after high school graduation, her whole family was surprised.

"Hey, if she found a guy who'll have her," said Bob, who by that time was in his second year of college, "why not?"

"But she's too young," protested Mrs. Hogue, shivering in front of the space heater, on the bedroom phone.

"This may be the best thing that's ever going to happen to her," said Jimmy, who was in his freshman year at the same college as Bob and was sharing the fraternity house phone on the call.

"Let her go, sweetheart," said Mr. Hogue from the second phone in the unheated basement laundry, wishing he'd put on his cardigan. "The boys are right. Let's not stand in her way. She's never going to be . . . you know."

"Oh," cried Mrs. Hogue.

"No drama!" commanded Mr. Hogue, and Mrs. Hogue swallowed her tears with a slug of port.

"I got married today," Lily wrote in her diary.

The wedding was small—the immediate family, as most of the extended family were estranged in Oklahoma or had begun the ancestral line's early exit through the lightning strike and two murders. Mr. Hogue gave Lily away to the accompaniment of Bach's concerto, and Mrs. Hogue wept, despite a heroic swallowing effort. The two older brothers were stalwart and inexpressive, secretly relieved that another man was now responsible for their very strange and mostly inept sister. The youngest sister was gone—exiting even earlier than most Hogues after stealing Mrs. Hogue's car keys and taking a joy ride that, sans *deus ex machina*, ended in a crash when she was only fourteen.

CHAPTER 3

Lily Hogue felt like a Martian the first night of her marriage. But feeling alien was familiar, so she coped as best she could. She instructed Philip that anything was fine except touching her navel, and shrugging his acceptance, he began.

"How was it for you?" he asked when they were done.

Lily sought to be encouraging yet honest. "It was like having a very strong, short, throbbing baseball bat inside me."

Philip's eyebrows shot toward his hairline. "Did I hurt you?"

"No," lied Lily. "Thank you. Thank you so much. You are wonderful. It's just that you are large."

Philip resumed breathing with a self-satisfied grin.

"How was it for you?" asked Lily warmly, relieved that she had repaired her gaff.

"You are the most beautiful woman I've ever known," said Philip, who had only dated one other person—a Boston girl he didn't talk about. "Your breasts! Your breasts. They're beautiful, Lily."

"Thank you," answered Lily demurely.

"Don't worry. They say it takes a while to get used to it. Especially for the girl," said Philip, slinging an arm around her shoulders. "The good part is we have our whole lives to practice!"

And that's when Lily stopped breathing. Her heart raced, pounding so hard she was sure it showed through her chest wall. Her mouth went cardboard dry and her throat closed. To cover her insanity, she vaulted out of bed, nearly clocking Philip the way Trouble had once clocked her, and lurched for the bathroom. "Got to pee," she gasped and then coughed heartily, pretending to have a tickle in her throat.

Lily and Philip were honeymooning in a hotel—not far from where Lily will live when the Seventy-second Street subway is attacked—and the bathroom was spacious enough for her to splay her five-foot ten-inch frame on the floor between the toilet and tub.

Should I go to the emergency room, she wondered as she writhed. No. The cold marble floor seemed to shock her out of her terror and gradually she became aware that she was breathing and was not in fact having a heart attack. Cold floor therapy. Good to know. If only her diary were in here, she could record the event. Perhaps she should find a hiding place for writing materials in their bathroom once they had their own place.

What would Philip do if she asked for a divorce? And where would she go? The plan had been to come to New York City so Philip, who had starred in several high school and community theater plays, could go to acting school. She supposed she could still get a secretarial job as planned. She certainly would not go home to her parents, to a family she had longed to escape. Her earliest memory after learning to write was at age six, carefully printing her will on the underside of the wood chair in her room: "I leave all my toys to Kristofer"—her pet turtle who fled his plastic volcano container as fast as a three-inch mail order turtle can and was never seen again.

She breathed deeply, concentrating on how she had gotten to where she was.

She had been the assistant stage manager for her high school's senior play, when Philip, a Boston transplant, auditioned using "Man of a Thousand Voices" Rich Little's impressionist routine that he'd copied off the Johnny Carson show, but in his version, Carson, Jimmy Stewart, and Dean Martin all sounded like Bostonians with pinched noses. He was cast as an understudy and Lily had felt so bad for him that she was more communicative than usual.

"How'd you learn all those words?" she'd asked him, standing in front of the callboard with the casting list where he'd just gotten the bad news.

"Oh, it's not hard," said Philip. "I guess I was too funny though—not quite right for *The Glass Menagerie*. I should've done something more serious. Hey, you want to go to the movies with me this Saturday?"

"I don't know," stammered Lily.

"You don't know?"

"Um. Yes. Yes, I could go to the movies. What do you want to see?"

"Whatever's playing at the Victoria—that's our only choice, right?" Not like where I come from."

"Boston?"

"Beantown!" he yelled, grabbing her hand and swinging it like they did this all the time. "I'll call you."

All day Saturday, Lily tried on outfits and hyperventilated. Philip never called. Monday, when she saw him in homeroom, he suddenly remembered, turned bright red, and slapped himself upside the head.

Lily liked having a boy interested in her. He didn't ask her to wear his name bracelet, but he'd stroll easily with her down the halls between classes and casually sit down at whatever table she chose in the cafeteria. Up until Philip, Lily usually sat at any table with at least two girls, and although they would acknowledge her, she was never included in their conversations.

Even so, the senior prom was Philip and Lily's first official date.

"I shall buy a dress," she'd told him.

She wore a light blue Sears cotton gown with a lace bodice, a rayon chiffon skirt, a dark blue satin sash that tied in a back bow, and matching shoes, $35.00 special ordered by Mrs. Hogue. "Mother says the blue brings out my eyes, even behind my thick lenses," she wrote in her diary.

Where were her eyeglasses? Lily sat up on the cold marble hotel bathroom floor and felt around for the toilet paper, pulled off a long piece, and blew her nose, emitting a strangled honk as she strained to eject the gunk from the back of her sinuses.

The night of the prom, she'd been fighting her many allergies. Her eyes were rheumy behind her lenses and they'd fogged up whenever she blew her nose. She'd spent the evening trying to unobtrusively wipe the eye run-off, and by the end of the dance, her mascara had resembled vampire makeup.

Philip had looked perfect in his tailored white tux with a blue bow tie that brought out his sparkly azure eyes. His yellow hair was cut but retained just enough of a tousle to make him look unselfconscious. His crooked-tooth grin immediately charmed Mr. Hogue and seduced Mrs. Hogue, who was so flustered that all she could say to Lily when she saw them off was, "That dress was worth every penny."

Even if she was a little different from the other girls he'd known, Philip found irresistible the way Lily would stare at him with what appeared to be admiration—pretty much no matter what he did. (It would be many decades until he realized this look meant she was having trouble seeing.) Just greeting her in the morning at homeroom elicited such adoration that it made him blush. The fact that Lily was practically legally blind without her glasses, to Philip, was charming—the way she'd suddenly get discombobulated if she was without her eyeglasses. The way she'd grope, laughing at herself, when they went in the community swimming pool. That was when they first kissed. Philip had an arm around her to guide her back to their towels. "Lily," he'd said, overwhelmed by her body in a one-piece, "I *like* you blind. You are so beautiful without your glasses and I'm such a lucky guy that you take them off in front of me." He was sure if she got contacts, other boys would see what he saw, so he quickly added, "but you're just as pretty in them, so you should probably wear them all the time."

When Philip opted out of college and declared his goal to become a standup comedian, his mother—a single mom who had divorced her husband in Boston—said, fine, but he still needed to get some formal training. Lily's bottomless adoration boosted his self-confidence, which feeling he mistook for love.

It had never occurred to Lily that she would have a boyfriend, let alone a husband. She enjoyed being with Philip and was first enamored and then soothed by the automatic social acceptability of having a partner. He was just the right amount taller than she was. Everyone responded to his crooked-tooth grin. He was kind, and that more than compensated for his basic laziness, lack of talent, and general stupidity, which in some way balanced her disconnectedness and made her complete lack of ambition seem all right. A *B* student, it had never occurred to her to go to college. She'd had no interest in her brothers' relentless competition, her father's mysterious comings and goings, or her mother's dedication to servility and port. When Lily sat in her room staring into space, repeatedly listening to the concerto on the little Victrola she'd gotten for her birthday—an activity her brothers never tired of mocking—what she was actually doing was trying to leave her body, at least in mind. Even if she never disappeared into the bliss of her first time, in her mind, she was in an unknown future where there were no other people. She imagined herself in a cozy room with warm colors, beautiful old furniture, a colorful rug, and sun pouring in from all directions—windows on all walls, a skylight maybe. Even though it was indoors, there was a feeling of nature, although she saw no plants. And it was quiet. Silent, even. In this fantasy mind room there was no family, no squabble, no repressed hostility, no pretense or competition or the possibility of it. She never thought about work or friends or money or any of the things that might cross one's mind when considering the future. She thought only of re-experiencing the blessed peace of Bach. But it never came.

"Will you marry me?" Philip had asked. "I'm 4F cause of my asthma and lousy feet, so I'm not leaving you for Vietnam. Plus, I'm a good cook and I'm pretty tidy, so you won't have to be like your mom. We'll get two rooms so you can have your alone time. I don't think that your liking to be alone and playing the same record over and over is weird. I'm not like your brothers. My dad will pay the rent for the first year and give us an allowance, so basically you can do whatever you want while I get my standup career going. I don't want to start this alone, and I really do think I might love you, Lily. Come with me to New York. If you want, you can divorce me after the year."

It was a proposal she could not refuse.

CHAPTER 4

"**S**o what do you think?" asked Philip, who'd just done his impression of Neil Armstrong deboarding Apollo 11 and walking in green cheese. "I'm thinking of adding sound effects."

Lily and Philip had lived for one month in their sparsely furnished, three-room apartment on West Eighty-first Street just off Amsterdam where the night quiet was often interrupted by the *pop-pop-pop* of shootouts, followed by screaming sirens.

Lily thought seriously about her response. She knew Philip had self-esteem issues and his confidence was shaky after getting booed off stage by the two audience members during the last set of open mic night at the dive around the corner where he was testing his material. "What if Neil Armstrong found a mouse in the green cheese?" she suggested. "And he could be afraid."

"You mean like this?" Philip hopped up on their secondhand couch with his fingers up by his chin, like a spastic cartoon girl.

"That's very funny," pronounced Lily.

"Okay, it's in. Thanks, sweetheart." And Lily blushed at the endearment.

That night, while Philip was at the comedy club, Lily began to plan. She had been working as a temp secretary in offices all over Manhattan. She was a good typist, but mostly her job was to occupy the chair of whichever secretary was out. So she could indulge her love of staring—as long as she directed it at a book and occasionally turned the pages.

What do I want? she wrote in her diary.

To be safe.

To be comfortable.

What do I want that I don't have?

A job that I like.

Paradise.

A reason to exist as opposed to the alternative.

What, in everyday life, do I like?

There was the problem. Lily sat and stared. She stared at the empty beige walls of the living room, the buzzing refrigerator, and the decrepit stained sink that marked the kitchen on the east wall, the blue shower curtain that separated her alone-time room from the north end of the living room, the mirrored door to the bathroom where Philip stood for hours practicing faces and moonwalking, and the open beige door to their tiny bedroom. She stared at the living room's meagre furnishings—the battered metal folding table that served as their dining area, a tufted gray sofa and two matching chairs from Philip's mom's basement, a secondhand TV that only showed a picture if you held the antenna. Philip was not interested in decorating since they'd only be here a year and, until this moment, Lily had not noticed furnishings or the details of any environment. And suddenly noticing what she had never noticed gave her such a shock that she popped out of the tufted gray side chair and the room seemed to rebound from her energy.

At four a.m., when Philip got home from the club, he was surprised to see Lily fully dressed, sitting upright in the tufted gray chair like it was noon. "You're awake," he said, pleased.

"How'd you do?" asked Lily.

"I killed," said Philip. "There were only three people plus the bartender for my set, but they smiled a lot when I did the mouse bit."

"Great," said Lily. "I think we need to do something about this apartment."

Philip looked at her funny. "Listen, it's four o'clock. Could we maybe talk about this in the morning?"

"Certainly," replied Lily, and they both prepared for bed.

CHAPTER 5

After only a few hours' sleep, Lily is not at her best for her temp job—a long-term placement in the public relations department of the Museum of Modern Art—but she sits alone in a room from nine to five where she does not worry about making a bad appearance. She has seen a couple of other temps who work on other floors. One looks like an overweight clown dressed in various over-the-top colorful costumes—Zelda something. And the other, a shy girl named Leslie, dresses like she's planning a day on a playground. After all of Lily's efforts to dress in proper office attire, her boss doesn't seem to even notice her. He prefers to pile up the work for his regular assistant who is out for several weeks recovering from corn surgery. "You won't mind," he told her when she'd started the job a week ago. "It'll be an easy month. Just answer the phone and tell anyone who wants me that I'm out at a meeting. Take a message." Then he disappeared with a small suitcase.

Like several MoMA business departments, PR occupies a number of rooms in a brownstone opposite the museum on West Fifty-fourth Street. A few years from now, rumors will fly that, from this building, connected to the museum via a secret underground passageway, the former governor of New York, Nelson Rockefeller, was hauled down a tunnel in order to avoid being found dead of a heart attack in *flagrante delicto* in one of the brownstone offices.

But right now, none of that has happened, and Lily, dead tired after waiting up for her comedian husband who provided no relief from her realization that she has never known where she is, let alone *why* she is, is studying the office, unsure why she feels embarrassed—as if she's intruding somehow—but she is determined to see the details. Not only see, but notice how they go together to form the picture that is called "office," find and name the patterns of the entities of desk, chair, fax, file cabinets that form this place where she is spending eight mind-numbing hours a day doing nothing.

"Are you all right, Lily?" asks Mr. Mason, her boss, on his way out with his small suitcase.

"I'm trying to see the design," answers Lily. "I've never noticed the art of rooms and I'm trying to see."

"Ah," says Mr. Mason, cursorily glancing at the relentless dirty beige that surrounds them. "Polly has never done much with her space. If you need a break from it, you know you can use your MoMA ID to go to the exhibits—even when the museum is closed—during your lunch break." And he picks up his suitcase and disappears.

At lunchtime, Lily bids adieu to the PR office walls, along with the strange feeling that she is never alone there and is in fact intruding on something she has no interest in knowing about, and she walks across the street to the museum. As she shows her ID to the guard, she starts to explain, but he clearly is not in the mood and he waves her through, along with other refugees from the PR building: fat Zelda, shy Leslie, a dark girl with strange eyes, and a nondescript person whom Lily doesn't notice. On entering the museum, all five go in different directions. *Temps*, thinks Lily. *We're all lost and temporary.* And with almost no interest in them or anything, she wanders from the entrance to room after room full of priceless art. She senses there is something she is here to see, but she has no idea what and has only forty-five minutes to find it. She can't remember last night's dream, but there was something . . . something . . . And there it is. She is the only one in the gallery. She zigzags almost dreamily, as if pulled to the Chagall. She's like a large metal body in water being sucked by a giant magnet to the other side of the room pool, to stand in front of a painting called "The Birthday."

First it's the warmth of the red carpet, the blues and green of the tapestries, the rich orange of the bedspread that draw her. See the pattern, she remembers. Center are two figures—a woman with a bouquet, in a black dress with a frilly white collar, being pulled, just as Lily is right now, but she's headed toward a window, and floating next to her, but above, is an armless man, a lover, his neck craned backward and twisted in an impossible position to catch her in a kiss. They float back to back, these impossible lovers, but in perfect harmony. See the shape of the sliver of white wall that shows between their bodies. It's almost a body itself, cutting off what would be a corner of the tapestry on the back wall as if it, too, is an entity. What is it about this painting? Lily is feeling faint and realizes she has stopped breathing. She draws in air and as she does, she could swear she sees the lovers move. The movement makes them inevitable. Back to back, but face to face, eye to eye, nose to nose, and mouth on mouth, they see each other, and they know they are not alone.

It is the most comforting picture Lily has ever seen, and she realizes she has been in a trance for forty-five minutes when her stomach growls and the noises of the public entering the museum shock her out of her reverie.

"What are we doing?" she asks Philip that evening as they eat his stove-top macaroni and cheese at the battered metal folding table.

"We're eating," he answers, flashing an open-mouthed grin.

"That's disgusting," says Lily. "You know I don't like gross faces."

"Sorry," he says and drinks his wine. "Sure you don't want some?"

Lily shakes her head and swallows a forkful of mac and cheese. "I went to the museum today."

"That's nice," says Philip.

"I saw a painting of two people who are so in love that they fly. And the room that they're in is all warm with colors, and everything moves in the same direction, and it makes sense."

"Hey, I saw this guy on the subway today with a duck," says Philip.

Lily stands up.

"I was wondering if I got some kind of funny animal for my act—"

Lily emits a strangled moan.

"What?" asks Philip, alarmed. "I heard what you said: you saw a painting with nice colors. Do you want to decorate the apartment or something? Fine. Then decorate. Go out and buy matching stuff. Charge it to my dad. What's the problem?"

"I can't do this, Philip," she says with such gravity that Philip stops chewing. "I've never known what I'm doing. All I've ever done is space out and run away. But I've never run *to* anything. I need to run *to* something and it's not us. Not even for a year."

"So?" says Philip, sincerely confused. "At least I got you out of your parents' house. We could have a baby if you want."

And that's how the marriage ends.

CHAPTER 6

What do I want?

Lily ponders the answer to this question for months, staring at the blank page of her diary, after she leaves Philip and moves into a drab flower-wallpapered room with a sink in an East-side rooming house on a floor with four other tenants and one bathroom. The assignment at MoMA extends into a second month when the regular assistant decides to have the corn on her other foot removed and then both she and Mr. Mason quit with no notice. Rumor is they are going away together even though Mr. Mason is married. Perhaps that had something to do with the small suitcase he carried when he left the office. Perhaps it has to do with whatever they did when they were both in the office. Lily wonders if she somehow felt this and it was the cause of her embarrassment. The museum asks Lily to man the office—just answer the phone and take messages until they hire a new director. And when the assignment ends, Human Resources calls her in to talk.

While Lily waits in H.R. reception, she ignores the other occupants: fat Zelda, shy Leslie, the strange dark girl, and the nondescript person she never sees. Nobody speaks. Finally, the head of H.R. calls her in, asks Lily various oblique questions about working at MoMA, seems satisfied with her "I like it very much" responses, and then turns cagey.

"Would you be comfortable working in a position where you would report back to us about your boss?" asks the head of H.R. "We've received some reports of problems and we just need to see what's true."

Mystified, Lily cannot think of a reason why she wouldn't be comfortable. After all, H.R. okays her time slips and is in a sense her supervisor. "That would be fine," she answers in her most pleasant work-appropriate secretarial tone.

And H.R. places her in the annual fund office where she prints the same fundraising letter over and over, changing only the recipient's name, and observes her boss. MoMA is a progressive institution that will not brook the employee abuse reported by the previous secretary—whose vitriolic all-caps note "FROM ROCHELLE; TO: WHATEVER UNLUCKY PERSON IS SITTING HERE NOW" Lily finds on the memory typewriter's hard drive, promptly deletes, and never reports to H.R. Lily's assessment: The former employee sounds insane and the boss, who shows no sign of the sadism or racism mentioned in the letter, is extremely disorganized with no memory for names and probably is suffering from what will eventually be referred to as a learning disability that she is desperately trying to hide. But unlike Mr. Mason, she is there, so Lily delivers to H.R. a benign report without mentioning any of her theories about the complicated psychology of everyone in the department who appears just as idiosyncratic and self-involved as the boss. Lily does not like complications. She avoids inter-office anything and every day at lunch, she visits the Chagall painting and ignores the other temps who, like her, vanish into the galleries.

After leaving Philip, Lily sees "The Birthday" differently: the lovers look older now. They probably have grown children. Lily has never envisioned herself as a mother. Not once. She doubts her mother ever seriously desired to do what a mother does, but she had no choice, being born in the 1920s. Lily is living in the midst of the feminist revolution. Just last week, hundreds of women marched down Fifth Avenue declaring their right to do whatever they want. Lily watched with the other spectators. She has known she can do what she wants since she left Philip, and her family, preoccupied with horse activities and cleaning, seemed content that she didn't need anything from them. She just wishes she knew what she wants.

The rooming house is a four-story building in the Yorkville section of Manhattan. Mrs. Schultz, the landlady, occupies the first three floors, including an ornate, old-world, wood-paneled parlor floor with her Persian rugs and many scarred antiques, many ever-changing visitors from Germany, innumerable elderly cats, and weekly spirituality discussion group gatherings.

Lily's floormates are: Sheba, whose real name is Margaret Scully, a California transplant who is trying to be a Broadway star, but who thus far has succeeded only in waitressing at Schrafft's on Seventy-ninth

Street between Lexington and Third; Sheba's younger sister and room-mate Elsie, who goes as Elsie, who is working as a legal typist; and, in the other double room, Ernie Shoren and his brother Ed from Wisconsin.

All four boarders are determinedly busy people, but Sheba is the busiest of all. She is not a good looking girl, but appears quite attractive due to her attention to her gleaming-toothed, welcoming smile; years before bleaching becomes the custom, she has discovered some method of whitening that will result in dentures when she is in her thirties. Nevertheless, the smile is effective in reducing both Shoren brothers to willing lackeys who move furniture, compete with each other to buy her dinner, and help with her myriad projects. There is always something—laundry, errands, rearranging her clothes—and whenever Lily sees her, she is warm, but in a terrible rush. "I have a very stressful life," she tells Lily, by way of explanation for having no time to say "hello." "After all, I really have two full-time jobs, what with waitressing and my acting. Do you think these earrings match my eyes?"

Lily nods sympathetically, hoping it addresses all of Sheba's non sequiturs, when they run into each other in the common first-floor kitchen. "My husband is trying to work in show business too."

Sheba's lips form a perfect *O*.

"We've separated," adds Lily quickly. "Slip of the tongue."

Elsie, too, is busy, but her goal seems less professional: finding a husband at her law office. Every night she returns to the rooming house dead tired and a little drunk after a day of typing followed by yet another dismal date. But she is intrepid and ever hopeful. "I want to get married, have a house in the country with a maid, and two children—a boy and a girl," she tells anyone in the house who will listen. When Sheba is in the vicinity, she rolls her eyes behind Elsie's back.

Ernie Shoren works at Bloomingdales as a store detective, prowling for shoplifters, and Ed is a stagehand at a West-side TV studio, driving a forklift that moves sets from one place to another. It is when he says it's for a soap opera that Sheba makes her choice: she will be in love with Ed, even though Ernie is the better looking of the brothers.

Lily watches these dynamics—the plotting and decisions—and she marvels.

Since none of the rooming house tenants are going away for the holidays, Mrs. Schultz suggests they join her and her spirituality discussion group for the Thanksgiving celebration. Sheba accepts as soon as Ed, whom she calls Eddie, says he thinks a house dinner is a cool idea, and everyone else follows suit.

"Vunderful," bubbles Mrs. Schultz. "Za discussion group vill be thrilled. Ve vill make together a feast!"

The sisters Scully are assigned a trip to the green market, but Sheba says, "Oh, that is a lifting job. Eddie and I will do that. Elsie, you won't mind switching, will you?"

Giving her sister an evil eye, Elsie Scully says fine, she'll go with Ernie to pick out the damned turkey. The sisters are just like Lily's brothers—always competing—observes Lily, who is alone for her assigned task. What is the point, she wonders as she shops for spices, herbs, ice cream, and beverages? What do you win? Sheba doesn't even like Ed, and if she manages to get a job through him on a soap opera, she will only demean the silly stories she has to act out, since she fancies herself a Broadway star. And what does Elsie think she will achieve if she gets some lawyer to marry her and move to the suburbs? All the suburban housewives Lily has ever known are like her mother. What is the point of anything?

Mrs. Schultz directed them to complete their tasks by Wednesday afternoon and be ready to prep in the kitchen at five a.m. Thanksgiving morning.

"What?!" said Sheba when Mrs. Schultz had handed her the list for the green market.

"It'll be fun," insisted Ed. "Cool, Mrs. S. We'll be fine."

"Well, if you say so," said Sheba dubiously, but quickly softening, realizing she's revealed her lack of domesticity and Ed has already told everybody how much he loves a woman who can cook.

So Thursday, in the black of early morning, the somnambulant and indolent little group of boarders converges in the rooming house kitchen.

"Chop!" orders Mrs. S, nodding at a row of cutting boards on the counter.

"Jeez," mumbles Sheba, "coffee first."

"Stuffing!" announces Mrs. S who has been here since four. "Needs onion, celery, sage sausage. There vill be my most famous green-bean casserole, midout disgusting mushroom soup. Only organic vegetables. Green yummy beans, onions on top. Candied yams mid syrup sauce, yum, mid brown sugar, honey, butter—lots of it—nutmeg, cinnamon, and one teaspoon chili powder. For dessert, za group brings pies. Many pies, all kinds. Chop, chop." And she turns back to her growing pile of turkey innards and shoves her arm up to her elbow inside the enormous bird.

"Sheba doesn't chop," whispers Sheba petulantly, pouring black coffee into her monogrammed mug with the flowers around the edge.

"Good god," says Elsie sliding past her in sheep-skin slippers that make her appear to be skating.

"Come on; it'll be cool," says Ed, planting himself in front of the pile of vegetables and chopping board.

Sheba smiles at Ed with practiced shyness as she places her mug out of danger's way and stands beside him so that her upper arm grazes his elbow. Ed is very tall. "I suppose it's good practice in case I ever play a wife," she says, gingerly picking up a chopping knife.

Ernie takes the board on the other side of his brother, next to Elsie who is already slaughtering a pile of mushrooms with far more energy than is required. And that leaves Lily.

Holiday preparations, and particularly those for Thanksgiving, were a heartless and sterile task in the Hogue household. Lily's father and siblings would disappear to the stable. Missing her dead mother, Mrs. Hogue would carefully measure out ingredients for dinner for nine. And then after the remaining grandparents' murder, heart attack, and breast cancer deaths, six. She never asked for Lily's help and Lily never offered, sensing that her mother took a mysterious pleasure in the hours of mourning, fussing, exasperated sighing, sipping port, and muttering non sequiturs such as "It's done" and "There's no love left."

At four o'clock the family Hogue would converge as if for an execution. "Happy Thanksgiving!" a puffy, red-faced, exhausted Mrs. Hogue would chirp, summoning a false brightness that the family responded to with the chewing and swallowing speed of competitive eaters. "Thanks; great meal," they'd say as they shoved away from the table and fled to the television, leaving Mrs. Hogue with the dishes.

This is a chance for a do-over, Lily realizes, as she surveys the disgruntled surrogate family scene in Mrs. S's kitchen. *I will participate.*

"Ow," squeals Sheba. "Oh, no!"

"What?" says Ed. "It's just a nick, for chrissake."

But Sheba moans and sways, waving her bloody pointer finger like Margaret Hamilton's wicked witch of the west "I'm melting" scene, practically forcing Ed to support her.

"We'll get a Band-Aid," he says to the kitchen and half-carries Sheba out of the room.

Lily takes their place at the cutting boards.

"Make sure no blood on za knife," orders Mrs. S, without missing a beat of whatever she is doing to the enormous bird.

Lily inspects, finds no blood, but nevertheless washes the knife, then joins Elsie and Ernie in joyless chopping. Sheba and Ed never return.

By four o'clock, when the discussion group members begin arriving with their pastries and pies and cakes, the whole rooming house is infused with delicious cooking aromas and Mrs. S and the boarders, finally including the elusive Ed and Sheba—who came downstairs at three thirty looking flushed and sheepish, Sheba displaying a finger wrapped in many layers of gauze—are finishing up the place settings at the many-leaved white-linen-clothed room-length dining table in the seldom-used formal dining room off the parlor.

Lily has changed into her one good dress, a green and wine-colored knit that her mother bought for herself in the last Sears order before Lily left home and Lily discovered next to her Crow blanket in her trousseau when she and Philip moved into their apartment.

"Happy Thanksgiving," greets Mrs. S, apple-cheeked and smelling of ginger.

The discussion group members hang and then pile their coats on the rack hooks in the vestibule, hug and kiss each other European style on both cheeks, and bustle into the kitchen to unload their food, as familiar as if they live here.

"Where are the kitties?" asks a dour-looking woman with a steel-gray pageboy and a severe mouth.

"Don't vorry, don't vorry," chides Mrs. S, scurrying to and from the kitchen with big serving bowls. "They have their goot dinner in za bedroom. Meet za boarders. Introduce yourselves. I be right in."

"Can't we help, Gretta?" offers an attractive man in his thirties, making no move to do so.

"No, no, Martin. Zat is Lily next to you. She is zingle."

Lily blushes several shades of crimson and removes her eyeglasses, cleaning a nonexistent smudge with the wine-colored sleeve of her knit dress.

She learns during dinner, when Martin is seated beside her, that he plays trumpet. She also learns that the discussion group members study the teachings of a dead philosopher and mystic named Gurdjieff, who taught that everybody is sleepwalking through life and to know yourself and thus become "awake!" you need to do work like seeing all your habitual behaviors and changing them, which is a real bitch, so mostly he just comes to the meetings for the company and snacks. But Martin says this part with a mouth full of turkey in a near whisper after drinking five glasses of wine. Then he invites Lily to come to the *Merv Griffin Show* where he plays in the band, and then later, go to a jazz club where they can hear some "real" music—not like the dreck they play at the Spirituality Discussion Club. He says not to repeat that last part to the rest of the group because they're a swell bunch and he likes coming and they—particularly Mrs. S, whom he calls "Gretta"—can get vicious if you question their methods or music, which may have diverged from Gurdjieff's original teachings, because divergence is in the spirit of Gurdjieff's emphasis on maintaining spontaneity in order to encourage a fluid, ever-changing morality which is more transcendent than any rigid notions of right and wrong, and Gretta is a true sage, psychic, and a damned good cook so he wants to stay in her good graces, and how about, after the jazz club, but only if she feels like it, maybe they can fuck?

CHAPTER 7

The line to get into the Ed Sullivan Theater snakes around Fifty-third Street and is filled with tense, chattering tourists gripping cameras, desperately trying to spot celebrities in the flow of people who are bypassing the line.

"Is *she* anyone?" Lily hears a pasty-faced man in a Stetson and a bolo tie say. His companion, also pasty-faced and a foot taller, squints at Lily through the lens of his Polaroid flash camera, then shakes his head in disgust.

Martin directed Lily to go to the front of the line and give her name to the doorman. "I'll put you on the list," he assured her.

"Martin who?" asks the doorman, slowly eyeing her legs.

"Martin Bratmore," says Lily, breaking the name into clear syllables. "He plays trumpet in the band. He said my name would be on your list."

The doorman, new on the job, doesn't know any VIP list other than the professional laughers, and Lily hardly strikes him as the boisterous type. "I don't want no trouble, Miss. Just stand here and shut up," he directs, jabbing his thumb at a spot behind him.

Lily sees that he is scared. She sees that he is angry at her because he is scared. There is something unaccountably familiar about him and she stifles an impulse to comfort him. He looks like the New York Jewish comedians Philip hangs out with, and probably he *is* one and he's angry at every single person in this crowd of desperate sycophants. And what they're all so angry or desperate about is that they are on the outside, waiting to get in. Why aren't they on the inside with Merv Griffin and his famous guests? It's not fair. And even worse, all is not fair even on the outside, because there are the Shebas of the world who may seem like they are on the outside, but between them and the doorman and the people in this line is a Grand Canyon-size gap. The Shebas of the world know that it's just a matter of time until lines form to see *them*. They know because they also know they will do anything to achieve entrance to the inner enclaves. *Anything*! Lily sees all this, shuts her mouth, and waits behind the doorman as directed.

When the door is opened, others protest as he sends Lily in, but they quickly are overwhelmed by being on the inside and they forget about it. Lily is pushed up the stairs by the current of people behind her. On the second floor, they flow like rapids into the cavernous pool of the studio theater where they are quickly directed into seats by an army of ushers.

Lily is seated in the front balcony when the stage manager directs everybody to shout and clap for the warm-up comedian who will come out momentarily and needs their help.

The warm-up man looks like an even angrier version of the doorman. Philip told her about these jobs—coveted by comedians. But from what she can see, it has more to do with dictatorial cheerleading. Sneering, berating, and running all over the stage, the warm-up man yells at the audience for not making enough noise and then he tests their laughing ability, sending them into gales of laughter so false it makes everybody laugh for real. By the time the show starts, her throat is sore and her hands sting from forced expressions of joyful appreciation.

Arthur Treacher, Merv Griffin's announcer and sidekick, radiates British disdain and looks as if he'd rather be home in a tub with a martini than sitting like a mannequin next to Merv. Merv Griffin is jolly throughout. He interviews a movie star Lily has never heard of, a famous British raconteur with a new book about losing weight, and an up-and-coming Broadway singer. Lily can barely see Martin who is behind the piano and a trombone player.

"You were wonderful," she rehearses as the show ends and the audience around her clears, receding out the doors like flood waters. The usher starts to insist that she vacate her row, when Martin's voice rings out from stage left: "She's with me!"

They don't go to dinner. Or the jazz club. Martin buys Chinese takeout and they go to his one-room apartment, a dingy walk-up on West Forty-third Street, across the street from a porn movie house. It is even more meagerly furnished than the apartment on West Eighty-first Street: a card table, no couch, no upholstered anything, a TV on a second card table, a torn poster of Charlton Heston dressed as a gladiator on the bare brick wall, and a mattress. On the floor by the mattress is a stack of books and magazines. As Martin preps for their meal, Lily examines the titles. The top book is about Gurdjieff's "Fourth Way." It's very dangerous, says the book jacket copy. It requires risk, sacrifice, or changing your embedded habits—changing your ideas about who you are. "Do you really want to change?" it asks in bold type.

The next book in the pile is a paperback called *The Art of War* by Sun Tzu. She picks it up, just to do something with her hands, since Martin has refused her help with the Chinese food. In the front of the book is a list of quotes:

> "The art of war is of vital importance to the State. It is a matter of life and death, a road either to safety or to ruin. Hence it is a subject of inquiry which can on no account be neglected."

> "All warfare is based on deception."

> "If you know the enemy and know yourself, you need not fear the result of a hundred battles. If you know yourself but not the enemy, for every victory gained you will also suffer a defeat. If you know neither the enemy nor yourself, you will succumb in every battle."

"Are you enlisting or something?" asks Lily, dropping the book back on the stack.

"What?" says Martin. "Oh. Funny. You like spicy, right?"

"Anything is fine," says Lily. "I'm going to wash my hands."

"Be my guest," says Martin, watching her head for the bathroom. "Don't look at the tub though. It's not my fault!"

After closing the door and flicking the light switch, Lily peers behind the closed shower curtain. The tub is more rust than enamel. She washes her hands and rejoins Martin at the card table. "So, *are* you?" she asks.

"Am I what?" answers Martin, chivalrously pulling out a folding chair for her.

"Thank you. Joining the military. You're reading a book about war."

"Good god, no," says Martin. "I'm a pacifist with a ridiculously high lottery number, and I've got flat feet and twitchy legs—lucky me. Chopsticks or fork?" He holds up the take-out selections.

"Fork please. Metal, not plastic."

"An iconoclast!" exclaims Martin, smiling.

"Or maybe I should change my embedded habits and use chopsticks— just to see if I turn into somebody else."

Martin chortles. "Another comedian." He hunts through a jar of miscellaneous flatware and hands her a stainless steel fork. "I like you the way you are."

"But you're trying to change, right?" says Lily, discreetly wiping a stain off the fork with several takeout napkins. "How exactly does that work? I mean what do you do in the Discussion Club?"

"We observe," says Martin, cryptically. "We observe the truth and we tell each other what we see. When I observe you, I—"

Adrenaline shoots through Lily's stomach. "Have you ever played classical music, Martin? Mmm, this is good."

"Sure," says Martin, watching her discomfort and enjoying it. "I play whatever pays."

Lily ignores the fact that he's smiling with a mouthful of noodles, just like Philip used to. It must be a male thing to think this is funny.

"Did you ever play Bach?" she asks, to avoid the topic of what he's observing. "Not that I know anything about music. But there's a piece by Bach I've always liked."

Seeing his opening—Lily's longing and confusion—Martin swallows quickly, turns serious and sincere, and leans in over his noodles. "If you love Bach, you must really understand things—pain, life, the heart. Bach was a genius. It takes wisdom beyond the intellect to fully appreciate that. Beethoven called him 'the immortal god of harmony.' I'll bet you like the romantic concertos, huh, Lily?" And he gets up so fast, Lily opens her mouth mid-bite and drops a noodle.

"Oh, excuse—" she starts, but Martin hasn't even noticed.

"I have the concertos here somewhere," he says, rifling through the shelf of LPs that runs the length of the room along the floor. "I keep them alphabetical, so you'd think I could— Ah! Here." And carefully, tenderly, he removes a thirty-three–and–a–third vinyl record from its sleeve. Fully aware of Lily's fixation on his hands, he caresses it as he moves to the stereo. Gently, so gently, he opens the top of the stereo with his left hand as he balances the record on the tips of his right fingers. Lily knows this is a dance of seduction and is mesmerized. Completely ignoring her, he seems enamored with the dinner-plate-size disk. He stares at it as if it is a great work of art or a woman's breast. He leans close, seeming to see a speck of something on one of the tracks, and he purses his lips and blows on it. Then with great respect, he lowers the disk onto the turntable, presses the "on" button, and watches as the automatic arm lifts and lowers the needle onto the first track. "Violin Concertos," he almost whispers, finally turning toward Lily, who has stopped breathing, her fork frozen midair, dripping noodles.

Through the first two concertos, tracks one through six, they finish their oil-drenched noodles and small helpings of Moo Goo Gai Pan and Diced Vegetable and Almonds, Lily mentions that she is estranged from her husband, and Martin's eyes register a *click-click-click* like an adding machine completing a calculation whose sum is a half-smile. During the seventh track, Martin silently toasts Lily—his beer bottle to her Coca Cola glass of tap water. And during the eighth track—the Largo Ma non tanto Double Violin chase, pursuit, and final love-making—Martin follows suit. Lily melts and together they swoon and roll and finally loll on his mattress on the floor.

"Thank you," says Lily, sitting up and searching for her underwear amongst the rumpled sheets and grateful that he never went near her navel even though she neglected to inform him of the rule.

"You *know* things, Lily," says Martin, smiling up at her, his hands cupped behind his head as he enjoys the view. "I mean you knew exactly how I like it. It was like you were inside my mind."

Lily smiles despite knowing that this is a line. "Oh. Well, that's good, I guess. Right?"

"It's like you're psychic," says Martin, without blinking, letting the words out on a long exhale. "You probably are like that with everyone."

"Well, I hardly—" starts Lily, reddening with horror.

"No, no, you misunderstand, sweetheart."

Sweetheart. Why does that endearment always stop her thoughts?

"I mean you're a 'knower'—one who *knows* how people work, who they are, what they feel. Like Gurdjieff or Bach or Gretta."

"Gretta?"

"Mrs. Schultz. Your landlady. I never was sure of this psychic stuff, but after this—" He gestures to himself and Lily. "You *knew*. You *know* me. *Me*. Without me saying anything."

Lily considers this. She considers Martin. He reads war books. Like her brothers and father, he is a man who must win. All her life she has longed for the paradise she once knew, disappearing into Bach. It's the only thing that's ever made sense to her, yet so elusive. She had an orgasm with Martin, but she hardly disappeared. She saw what he wanted. He'd signaled everything—with a gesture, a moan, a turn of his body. His erect penis sent out energy directing her from its tip to the beginning. There was nothing psychic about her knowing. She just followed the obvious connections. But she knows he knows that she feels so lost, so alien, so without purpose that it might seal his win by praising her rare talents now. "That is very sweet of you to say, Martin," she answers, slipping into her bra and reaching for her dress. "I'm flattered. Maybe I could hang out a shingle and tell fortunes." She stands, finds her shoes, and straightens her skirt.

Martin now is mesmerized. "You knew I was throwing you a line just now. Didn't you?"

"Thank you for a lovely evening, Martin," says Lily, slipping her purse strap over her shoulder.

CHAPTER 8

When Lily returns to the rooming house after her date with Martin, there is a note taped to her door: "Call your mother." She'll do it tomorrow when she can use the free MoMA long distance line, but as she's standing outside her door contemplating the note, Sheba and Elsie open their door and, in an uncustomarily friendly exchange, tell her that they took the message and hope nothing bad has happened.

"Excuse me?" says Lily.

"Your mother sounded upset," says Elsie, masking gossip hunger as concern.

"She drinks," answers Lily, opening her door. She is weary from Merv Griffin and casual sex, and the only thing she wants is to drop into bed and disappear into sleep.

"She said it was an emergency," says Sheba. "I think you should call her back."

"Hi, Mother; it's Lily. I got your message. What's the matter?" murmurs Lily into the downstairs parlor phone, aware that the Scully sisters have probably followed her and are huddled on top of the second-floor landing eavesdropping.

"Lily?" shrieks Mrs. Hogue.

"Yes, Mother, it's me," says Lily, cringing away from the ear piece. "What happened?"

It takes several minutes to understand through the sobs. It was a freak accident. Mr. Hogue and his two sons had been riding together on the trails overlooking the cliffs. There was a fall—Mr. Hogue and Trouble off the side of one of the narrowest passes. Bob went after him. Then Jimmy. Only the two rented horses survived. The bodies were discovered and the story pieced together after the horses returned to the stable on their own.

"Yes, I'll come home, Mother," whispers Lily, breathless. "I'll take the first train in the morning.

"There's nobody left," moans Mrs. Hogue, rocking with her skinny arms wrapped around her torso. "First your sister, and now everybody else." She rocks and moans and drinks.

Lily feels as if she has no blood in her body and breathing is no longer an autonomic function. She is sitting on the side of her mother's bed as Mrs. Hogue keens, doubled over her dressing table so that she can watch her pain in her makeup mirror.

"I don't know what to do. What do I do, Lily? My whole family is gone and I look like a hag."

Lily swallows hard. "I'm here, Mother."

"Of course, of course, but you know what I mean."

Lily stares out the bedroom window into the bleak, early-winter brown of the untended backyard where a deer is nosing around the dormant tulip bed searching for anything edible. If her father were around, he'd run for his rifle. She remembers his explosive energy as he'd call the boys and order the kill. "You know," she says without taking her eyes off the deer, "I was always afraid of Father. The boys, too, when they turned into his army. Maybe it was just time for that to be over."

A rippling heat shoots like a well-aimed bullet through the room and into Lily, shocking her attention back inside. "Lily Hogue, I don't know what's wrong with you," says her mother in a voice that can only be described as chilling. "I've always known you had . . . problems. But this! This! Your father and brothers are dead!"

"I just meant—"

"Listen to me, and listen hard," says her mother with sudden ferocious sobriety. "There are rules. You can't break the rules. Families, no matter how much you don't like it, stay together and support each other. That's all you have."

"But what if that's just a bad habit?" blurts Lily. "What if your family keeps you from being who you really are?" She gags on the last word as a laser beam of hate shoots from her mother's blue eyes into her own. "I mean where I'm living, they have a spiritual club where people actively try to change, and—"

"Quiet!" commands her mother, and Lily gulps. Her mother's face looks like white marble now, and only her mouth moves. "I'm going to tell you a story and then I never want to hear any of this insane talk again. Are you listening, Lily?"

Lily nods dumbly. Her mother has never told her a story. Not even when she was young.

"As you know, my parents divorced when I was twelve. It was a horrible thing. Not done at that time. Mother moved myself and your late Uncle Charles to a calm, middle-size town near where she'd grown up in Oklahoma and for four years, we did not see our father, who remained in our old house on Long Island. We had corresponded with Father over the years, but finally, to avoid the stigma of being children of a broken home, Mother decided we should go for a visit.

"To our surprise, we were met at the train station by a very thin man of about fifty, with a crewcut, dressed in stiff white Bermuda shorts, a frilly shirt, and steel-rimmed glasses."

Lily is stunned. Is there an invisible book somewhere? Her mother sounds as if she is reading. Or reciting something she's read and repeated over a lifetime. A script.

"I said, are you hearing this, Lily?" Mrs. Hogue almost shouts.

"What? I mean, yes. Go on. I'm sorry."

"I *hate* when you do that," huffs Mrs. Hogue. "Go off somewhere in your head. It's disrespectful." And then, dismissing it, she takes a sip of port and continues from where she left off: "It turned out Father's 'man'—Sal—was a member of a religious cult. For a week, he insisted in his high-pitched fluty voice, that we practice breathing exercises and strange poses every morning at five a.m. in order to tune in to high thought currents, he said. We, of course, thought the whole thing was a ridiculous charade, but we went through the motions to please Father, who clearly was . . . attached . . . to this strange man.

"Before we could eat our eggs and toast, the fellow insisted we lie on our stomachs on the floor, with the man straddling first Charles and then me and pinning our arms.

"'This is the position of review,' said Sal. 'While you lie here, try to review in your mind what your most important possessions are. Find your true nature!'

"He had us close our eyes and stretch our arms behind us while gripping our heels together. The higher he raised my arms, the more it hurt. But then suddenly something gave. The back of my neck didn't ache anymore. I suppose I simply got used to the position. My tense muscles relaxed and there was a peace, like a soft cloud, friendly and harmless. And I disappeared."

Lily feels as if she is going to explode. Her mother knew this feeling too—the Bach feeling, the softness, the disappearance. "I know that feeling," she whispers, but her mother holds up a hand for silence.

"Father came to me in secret. It is, I believe, the only time he shared a confidence with me. 'Don't take Sal seriously, sweetheart—'"

Lily's heart catches on the endearment—another thing she and her mother have in common?

"'I love Sal dearly, but he is . . . odd . . .,' said Father. 'I'm grateful that you humored his religious practices, but I would appreciate it if you didn't tell your mother about them . . . about him. About us.' There was a plaintive note in his voice. I will never forget it."

Lily's heart melts as she watches her mother disappear into the memory. And suddenly she is there too—in the memory, as if it is now.

"Father drew a long breath. 'I'd hate for your mother to find you, well, changed in any way.'"

"But you *are* changed!" interrupts Lily, feeling like an ethereal being screaming to her mother's deaf child self. "You feel the peace."

"No!" snaps Mrs. Hogue. "Listen to what Father said: 'No! No!'" she booms. "'Tell your mother nothing. This is very important. Do you understand?'"

Lily isn't sure if her mother is asking her if she understands or is still quoting her father. So she says nothing, mesmerized by her dual vision of her adult mother and the child version.

"There was a genuine fear and need in Father's face," continues Mrs. Hogue. "I was to say nothing of this strange man in a ruffled blouse and return to normal. 'Say nothing of the practices,' said my father. 'Do you promise?' At the time, I did not understand, but I wanted to make him happy, so I promised. 'Remember, you haven't changed a bit,' he reminded me as he loaded us on the train back to Oklahoma.

"As the train rolled out, Father waved with one hand back and forth slowly across his face, with Sal standing primly beside him in his ruffled shirt and bermudas.

"During the long trip, I felt curiously lonesome, not belonging anywhere."

It's the nothing place, Lily longed to whisper.

"Charles ignored me. No one was in charge of me. Nothing but green hills and telephone poles and the next morning, the scene through the window had changed to the flat, dusty plains of Oklahoma, with the same telephone poles going by. It was less than an hour before we were to arrive, when I said to Charles, 'Where do you think I can do the position here—to find my true nature? In the aisle?'

"Well, Charles acted as if I had cursed. 'Stop this,' he said. 'You heard what Father said. Do you want to get Mother all upset? Don't you want Father to be happy? Just be as dumb as you've always been. Don't ever try to be anything else.'"

"Oh, Mother," moans Lily.

"He was right! Family is everything. You sacrifice for family, Lily."

"But, Mother, you could have found—"

"No!" booms Mrs. Hogue. "One must play by the rules. I could not have found anything—nothing I didn't find with my parents and then with your father. You would know that if you had ever really been part of this family. Have you never done anything you didn't want to do?"

Lily tries to answer, but it is like blowing into a tornado.

"No, of course you haven't. It has never even occurred to you. You have always been separate. When your sister died, it was the same thing. Just nothing."

"But, Mother, we weren't close. We didn't even talk."

"Because you're deficient. I don't know how it happened, Lily. I think you were born that way. Even as a small child, you were cold. Incapable of feeling. Incapable of love. It's no wonder your marriage fell apart." And then looking away, as if suddenly overwhelmed with despair, she carefully arranges an errant piece of hair. "It's probably my fault," she almost whispers. "After all, you were my mistake."

CHAPTER 9

It all began with a typo—an *N* instead of a *B*. Francine, the annual fund manager, does not like the upset of new people whose names she can never remember nor faces recognize—due to what, several decades from now, will be diagnosed as face blindness, or an inability to recognize faces, or prosopagnosia—so when Lily's temp agency told Francine that Lily would be out for two days due to personal matters, rather than replace her with a new temp, Francine made the revisions on the fundraising letter herself. It was a follow-up appeal to trustees and museum members who had not yet made a donation after receiving the first letter. With her revision, Francine sought to highlight past accomplishments enabled by generous donations, and the glitch came in the third paragraph. What she'd meant to write was how several of the support departments have "bigger staffs" due to donors' gifts. The letter *B* is right next to the *N*. Anybody could have made such an error—even somebody without undiagnosed dyslexia and multiple learning disabilities—and Francine apologized profusely and tried to explain this when the brouhaha exploded. The trustees, who were White, were inclined to understand and forgive. So was her supervisor. The problem came when the glitch became gossip among the office workers, many of whom were Black and had heard the former fundraising secretary's vitriolic allegations about Francine's disorganization and inability to remember her name or even recognize her with a courteous nod when they crossed paths anywhere outside the fundraising office, which the secretary interpreted as a clear case of "they all look alike" racism.

Lily knows none of this when she returns to her job as Francine's temp secretary three days after learning that her father and brothers are dead and her mother thinks she is deficient—defective. All she knows is that her boss, Francine, seems distraught when Lily knocks on her door for the morning instructions.

"Rochelle, I'm busy!" calls a congested voice from the other side of the door.

She sounds as if she's crying, thinks Lily, as she returns to her desk behind the trustee files, most of which have "Rockefeller" somewhere in their name. Didn't one of the Rockefellers own the land with the horse trails where her father and brothers got killed?

Yes! says a resounding voice in her head.

Why am I here? she thinks, hoping for more illumination.

No answer.

"Hey," says a voice just outside the doorway to the hall.

"Hello?" answers Lily, not entirely sure if the voice is real or in her head.

"Oh," says the woman, stepping in, then pulling back as if she expected someone else. "No problem." And she walks away. The woman is very beautiful in an artsy way. She wears an African-patterned dress, many silver bracelets, and a matching head scarf that makes her brown skin radiant.

There is audible, almost palpable tension seeping in from the hallway—sounds of feet scurrying, muffled conversations, whooshing noises. Lily tries to read one of the *Parabola* magazines she picked out of Mrs. Schultz's community magazine pile, but the articles are too lofty— what her mother would call "gobbledygook"—and her concentration is constantly pulled away by the sounds of barely suppressed fury in the hallway as well as an occasional plaintive sob from Francine's office.

During the morning, several other clerical staff stick their heads in the door. Lily has spoken to them in the employee cafeteria, but when they see her sitting in the secretary's chair, they uniformly look displeased and speedily exit.

At five minutes to twelve, Lily decides to try once more. "Francine?" she calls, after gently knocking on the closed office door. "Francine, it's Lily. If there's anything for me to do, I'm happy to do it, but if not, I'd like to go to lunch, if that's all right."

Silence. Then books falling. Then the distinct *tap-tap-tap* of Francine's high heels as she patters across the floor and opens the door. "I suppose you've heard," she says balefully. "I'm not a good typist and an even worse proofreader. I should have waited for you to come back. It was a mistake, but not a reason for a conspiracy of vitriol. I hope you were able to take care of your personal matters, and I'm sorry for all the turmoil. I have to go to H.R., but it's fine if you want to take lunch now."

All the long tables in the second-floor employee cafeteria are taken when Lily enters. And it looks like a strange kind of split tide of people: there is a small round table, like a whirlpool, by the tray dump populated by dark and medium-dark Black women. Some kind of intense meeting. There's the woman in the head scarf and several others who have looked into the office this morning. They all lean forward over their food, speaking in hushed tones and interrupting each other. As Lily heads for the only empty table in the room, adjacent to theirs, she cannot make out the conversation; just as the voices rise, somebody makes a "keep-it-down" gesture and a silence falls over the corner. Lily sits at the far end of the empty small table to give the women as much space as she can, and she opens her brown-bag lunch: the last of Mrs. Schultz's left-over turkey in a pumpernickel sandwich, which she insisted Lily take this morning, plus several Thanksgiving cookies and a small, round pastry from the discussion club. "Allow this," Mrs. S had said. "When you lose someone dear, allow others to feed you, yah?" Even though Lily is not a big meat or sweet eater, she saw what was behind Mrs. S's gesture and said "Thank you." "It's what we can do," said Mrs. S. "*You* do *us* a favor by accepting."

". . . reeks of white privilege—" hisses a loud voice from the Black women's table, quickly hushed by the "keep-it-down" gesture.

Turning pink, Lily unwraps her sandwich and wishes she were sitting anywhere but here. Maybe she should repack her sandwich and go to the frozen sculpture garden. Do they even allow food there?

"Mind if we join you?" says the fat temp Lily has ignored for months. Zelda. An oddly sharp, but bubbly voiced person it seems. And without waiting for a response, she, shy Leslie, the odd dark girl, and I—we all look about Lily's age (don't worry; I'll explain in a second)—we all drag out chairs, scraping them along the floor for maximum noise, seemingly oblivious to the scornful glares from the women at the Black table. "Zelda McFigg," says the fat girl, giving Lily an amused once-over as we all plunk into our chairs. "I know you've seen me around. Leslie Kove is the timid one over there, this dark weirdo is Harmony Rogers, and that one, I don't know. Betsy something? She never talks so nobody ever notices her. I guess it's about time we all met."

(Yes, I was part of this group—the omniscient first-person narrator on the first page of this book. Young, agog, fascinated.)

"I am not weird!" says Harmony, ignoring the quizzical looks of the Black women, knowing they are wondering what race she is and if she belongs at their table, but they will not be so blatant as to do anything more than look at her, signaling "If you're a sister, you belong with us." Harmony is used to such half-assed curiosity and ignores it. "And you are?" she asks Lily.

Harmony has strange eyes, thinks Lily, not immediately realizing the question is directed to her.

"Who are you?" prompts Zelda. "She wants to know your name, but her eyes move in different directions so you can't always tell who she's talking to. We've seen you around for ages—in the brownstone, in the galleries, at that weird H.R. interview. We're all temps. I assume you're one of us. Whatever prize we were vying for, apparently you won it at H.R. By the time they got to us, all they said was 'Sorry to have bothered you. We had a little problem but it's solved. Carry on.'" Zelda sinks her teeth messily into a jelly doughnut, biting off half and chewing, eyes still on Lily.

"Zelda is very rude," says Leslie, the timid one, stirring her pea soup from the concession stand and wondering if she should have gotten vegetable.

"It's my charm," says Zelda, without wiping the jelly off the side of her mouth. "Which agency are you from?"

"How do you know I'm a temp?" asks Lily.

All of us laugh.

"It seems this is the only empty chair," says an older woman—maybe fifty and languorously beautiful in an uncategorizable way. Not like MoMA-artsy in black clothes or leftist colorful chic, but something solely her own and a little mysterious. "I'm Lucresse," she says, smiling from one of us to the other. "Lucresse Briard. I'm new. Just in for the day, consulting. You all look like you're old hands at MoMA."

All of us laugh and introduce ourselves around the table.

The cafeteria feels like a world-weary mixer for pessimistic artistic intelligentsia, mostly in their twenties and thirties. Most wear black—patterned stockings with black boots and skirts for the women and black shirts with black jeans for the men. They are White, Asian, a smattering of East Indian, and light-skinned Black people who are actively ignoring the small swirling pool of dark and medium-dark Black women in the corner next to the tray dump. In the split tide of this room, the majority has pulled to the long-table side of the room by crowding extra chairs around those tables, creating a buffer zone with the table now occupied by Lily, Leslie, Zelda, Harmony, me, and now Lucresse.

We look like a garden of mismatched, one-of-a-kind plants that don't resemble the rest of the room: Lucresse, lithe and graceful like an iris in a casual yet corporate blue linen pants suit with a large flowered silk scarf; Zelda, squat and wide like a mushroom, in a pink thrift-store peasant blouse over an ankle-length, shapeless, equally pink skirt; Leslie, like a scrappy dandelion, in jeans and a bright yellow rayon over-blouse; Harmony, like a chimera orchid with mismatched wandering eyes set on an exotic dark face atop a body garbed in something nondescript, corporate, and dark green; Lily, like a long-waisted, near-sighted lily, appearing even taller in a pencil skirt, blouse, and ill-fitting blazer—all courtesy of Sears Roebuck; and me. (Patience. I'll describe myself later.)

"I'm doing a brochure for the education department," says Lucresse, biting into her cafeteria-bought chicken salad. "Where are you all working?"

"Publications," say Leslie, Zelda, Harmony, and I in a chorus.

"We're stuffing envelopes," says Zelda through a mouthful of food. "But I'm really an actress—Zelda McFigg, my real name thanks to my dear departed and demented progenitors, but perfect for a comedic character actor, don't you think?"

Leslie and Harmony quash smiles and look at their food.

"And the rest of you?" asks Lucresse, with no hint of amusement. "What are the rest of you 'really'?"

"I like to garden," says Harmony, mostly to fill the awkward silence.

"Sure, me too," lies Leslie. "Love those vegetables."

"I'm in the fundraising department and I have no idea what I'm doing here," says Lily and we all laugh with relief. Then all faces turn to me.

"I watch," I say. "I'm a watcher."

Zelda laughs theatrically, and a loud moan of displeasure arises from the Black women's table. Alarmed, Lily swallows her laugh and stares at her lunch.

"What?" says Zelda extra loud. "We're not allowed to laugh?"

"It's not that," mumbles Lily, sotto voce.

"Then what is it? It's like being happy violates MoMA rules or something. Nuts if you ask me," says Zelda.

"Who asked you?" says Leslie.

"Hey, hey," says Harmony, making the "keep-it-down" gesture. "Easy, okay?"

Lily softly clears her throat. "I think my boss is being fired," she almost whispers. "I think it has something to do with—" And she gestures toward the Black table with a subtle elbow move. "I don't know what it's about, but—"

"That explains everything," says Harmony.

Lily, Leslie, Zelda, Lucresse, and I stop eating mid-bite and wait for her to continue.

"I heard she was racist or something," says Harmony. "I don't know the details. Francine, right? In fundraising. I know where you work. I was just playing dumb to be polite."

On the word "racist," spoken at a near whisper, a hush falls over the dining room and all eyes from the women at the Black table turn toward Harmony.

Harmony blushes and avidly drinks Coke, even though she prefers Pepsi and the beverages dispenser was out. After a beat, the Black women resume their conversation.

"I don't think she's racist," says Lily softly. "Just really disorganized." We women look at her quizzically. "I mean in her brain. There's something wrong in her brain. The way she sees and hears. It's hard to describe."

"That could describe all of humanity," says Lucresse dryly and all of us erupt again in laughter.

"The problem with humanity," says Leslie, "is we're all scared shitless and trying to pretend that we aren't."

"Not me," says Zelda. "My only problem is I can't get a break."

Harmony finishes her egg salad and looks at her empty plate. "The problem with humanity is that they don't pick up nuance."

"How do you mean?" says Lily, who knows exactly what she means.

"You know exactly what I mean," says Harmony, and Lily blushes.

"Nuance," says Lucresse, savoring the syllables. "What a lovely, soft, many-layered word." And all of us laugh.

"Take color, for instance," says Harmony loudly, with a sudden desire to cause trouble. "Take white," she continues with a tickle of a twinkle in her big, hazel, roaming eyes.

Leslie, Lily, Zelda, Lucresse, and I come to attention. As do the women at the Black table.

"White," says Harmony, as if nothing special has happened, "it's made up of all different colors, but we don't have the nuanced vision to see them. So most people just see white. Or black. Glaring differences. They base all their decisions—their movements, if you will—on these un-nuanced perceptions: we're no different from other animals, the way we'll suddenly fly off or stampede or do whatever the herd is doing."

Everybody is holding their breath.

"Except for me, of course, because I was born nuanced."

The Black women make a communal *humph* and go back to talking. Leslie, Lily, Zelda, Lucresse, and I stare at Harmony, waiting for her to continue.

She doesn't.

"So you see nuances?" asks Lucresse. "What do they look like?"

Harmony doesn't answer.

"I see nuances," says Lily finally, to fill the silence. "I see that nobody knows what they're doing but that it feels so awful not to know that we all try to hide it—by pretending to be what we're not, by 'the art of war' or by trying to win something, or by being right or being so sure that somebody else is wrong or bad and therefore we're virtuous and noble so that for a few moments we actually imagine we don't feel like a lost, wiggly speck among billions of similar specks writhing around on a big blue rock hurtling through what will eventually turn out to be a big black hole of vacuous nothing."

"Bummer," says Leslie. And we all laugh.

Due to the pressure of minority staff—all of whom deliver a signed letter following their furious lunch meeting, citing not only Francine's unforgiveable "typo" (giving her the benefit of their doubt), but her chronic obliviousness and rudeness, "which can only be characterized as insensitivity and possible bias as concerns minority support staff," as well as her "demeaning habit" of requiring such staff to wear nametags at fundraisers—treating them like "chattel," Human Resources has no choice but to relieve Francine of her duties as annual fund manager, which in turn relieves Lily of her job, so no need to finish out the week, her temp agency informs her.

CHAPTER 10

Holidays are an excellent example of un-nuanced human herd movement. The calendar, an arbitrary measurement, hits a certain marker, and en masse the herd decides to act festive.

Lily's mother had informed her that she's sold the house and Christmas will be a good time for Lily to come collect anything she wants from her room. Trying to ignore the sudden sense of suffocation, Lily promised to come. But two days before she is due to take the train, one of Mrs. Hogue's neighbors calls, tearfully informing Lily that there's been a terrible accident.

"What hospital is she in?" asks Lily, blasting through her reluctance to be a decent daughter. After all, she is her mother's only family.

"She's gone, dear," says the neighbor. "I'm so sorry."

And Lily will keep her reaction a secret for the rest of her life. Yes, she is numb, devastated, and a little terrified. She cries for a week, hard sometimes, but the tears are complicated: She is also relieved that it's over. Finally, no more obligations to a family she's never been comfortable in.

"I will not ever go home again," she writes in her diary.

There is nothing from the house that she requires, and even though she is not yet showing, she is relieved that she will not have to explain her pregnancy. She has been debating whether to even tell Martin, whom she has not seen since the night of Merv Griffin, but when Mrs. S, who is quietly sympathetic to her loss, invites her to join her Spiritual Discussion Club meeting on Christmas eve, Lily accepts—for the company but also to see what she feels when she sees Martin again.

The Scully sisters and the Shoren brothers have made out-of-town Christmas plans, and it will be nice to have a quiet house, a small gathering of people interested in mysterious things, and maybe have some time alone with Mrs. S to discuss her (Lily's) "situation." She senses Mrs. S will be open to the fact that she's already decided to keep the baby even though she has no idea how she will manage.

The topic of the Christmas Eve discussion club is "gratitude"—what is true gratitude and what is feigned or false, and how can we know the difference? Lily thinks about this while she dresses for the group. She chooses a loose-fitting pair of slacks and a bulky blue and green wool and cotton pullover. She stands on her desk chair in front of the bureau wall mirror so she can see her belly in profile. Almost flat. She believes she is truly grateful for this baby and for the fact that she doesn't yet show. Yes, she has never longed for children the way Elsie Scully seems to—even under all the manipulations and strategies to garner the right husband and house, there seems to be an authentic yearning. Lily has seen the way her eyes turn soft and sad when she spots a young mother with a baby carriage. Lily has never had this longing, but now that an actual person is growing inside her, she is not only grateful, but she feels such a fierce protective instinct that, for the first time in her life, she knows she is a killer. When the doctor at the clinic assumed she would want to "do something about it," a murderous rage erupted in Lily's gut and it was all she could do to keep from assaulting the woman.

Lily will appreciate this new little person no matter what he or she is like. It will be a surprise and she'll curiously await the emergence of the baby's unique personality and peculiarities. Whatever he or she wants, Lily will listen and say, "That's wonderful. How can we do that" or "get that" or "learn that?" She will never tell her child that he or she is without normal human capacities or is defective and a mistake. She will simply appreciate, encourage, and nurture. She'll learn to cook and she'll do everything and anything to protect this baby!

Perhaps they'll move out of the city. Certainly she can find a job with her orderly nature and good typing skills. In a smaller town with a job, she will probably find friends. She'll change! Starting fresh, she will be whoever she chooses. She can tell people her husband died in Vietnam—a small lie to avoid rumors and the unnecessary label of "bastard." She'll find a little house. Since she is her mother's only heir, she presumes she will receive some money from the house sale. She'll have to look into all that with Mrs. Hogue's neighbor, who was named executrix and has generously offered to handle her mother's affairs. Yes, she'll have a little house and a little baby and maybe a little dog. She always wanted a dog rather than a horse, but her father was neither pro nor con, so it was one of the few family decisions left to her mother and the last thing Mrs. Hogue needed, she explained to Lily when the others were at the stable, was another animal to feed and clean up after. Lily is grateful that her mother— . . . No, best not to express that thought . . . even in her diary.

"I think true gratitude is what I feel right this minute, being part of this wonderful group, here on Christmas Eve," says a dramatically red-haired woman in her forties, the first person to "share" at this evening's Spiritual Discussion Club. She crosses her leather-booted legs easily and leans toward the center of the circle, sweeping the group with twinkly eyes and a bright-toothed smile. "My children are with their father and I just don't know what I'd do without all of you. And, Gretta . . ." Her eyes fill with water. "I'm just so grateful. That's all." She waves at herself with long white-polished fingernails as if to staunch the overflow of feeling, her gaze directed first modestly down at her lap then flickering up—and that is the moment Lily knows that although this woman has all the earmarks of a grateful, vulnerable, single mother who does the best she can, given her circumstances, she is full of rage and every bit as dictatorial as Lily's father, the counterfeit general. Perhaps it is the kind of protective rage Lily is feeling for the baby, redirected into frustrated fury. The woman's "tell" is the calculation behind her nanosecond peek: Does the group adore her? Are they charmed? Are they on her side?

Lily waits to see if Mrs. S—Gretta—will say something.

Silence.

Martin hasn't come to the meeting—he'd phoned, Mrs. S said: something about his twitchy legs. Lily is surprised to realize she's grateful for his absence. The baby is the best thing that's ever happened to her and she has no wish to invite complications. But she will no more voice this than she would confront the red-haired woman who just spoke. There is no benefit to these kinds of frictions.

"Ve need to find gratitude in za heart," Mrs. S is explaining. "Can we describe za sensations in za body of this delicious feeling?"

An older man with hand tremors, a shock of thick white hair, and a reedy voice says that he is grateful for intellectual endeavors and that because he is able to read and contemplate the principles of consciousness and awareness, he feels grateful that he has a spiritual life that is so much richer than most people's.

"Ya, but za sensations," prompts Mrs. S, "in your body. Who has feelings in za heart or za tummy?"

One of the younger members of the group—around Lily's age—flaps her hand like an eager grade schooler. "Oh, I know what you mean," she blurts, without waiting to be called. "Sometimes, sometimes, like right after sex, it's like my whole pelvis floods with warm, flowy, hotty kind of stuff, and—"

"I really *want* to be grateful," interrupts a square-jawed man in his thirties, well dressed in casual work clothes—expensive shoes, perfectly tailored trousers, and a blue-grey cashmere sweater over an open-necked white cotton shirt. Probably he put his tie in his coat pocket as soon as he left his office. "I mean I do. I've got a great-paying job, a beautiful fiancée. I mean I've got all this stuff, so, yeah, I'm grateful, but I want more! I mean that's why I'm in this group. So yeah, sure, I'm grateful. Damn me, I'm a moron," he says, pummeling his forehead and grinning so that all the women in the circle blush.

Score! thinks Lily. He got his fix.

"I didn't have anything else to say anyway," mumbles the young woman with the hot pelvis who was interrupted; then she recoils into the back of her chair when nobody notices.

For the rest of the meeting, Lily feels like a Jupiterian. Like an alien life form that has awakened in a place she has never known and would never have imagined or believed existed had another Jupiterian tried to describe it to her.

Everybody is driven by a compulsive craving to get something. Even in a gathering about gratitude, the descriptions are spiraling attempts to charm, to be liked, to affect an appearance of goodness or sensuality or generosity or wisdom. And just like in Lily's family, once the threads of the story weaves are unspooled, the competition crackles and pops, floods and swirls—ever escalating to demonstrate superior feelings of gratitude. Lily feels as if she is drowning, like her every orifice is being filled beyond capacity with other people's denied vomit.

"Vat do you expect?" asks Mrs. S hours later as she and Lily wash dishes and put away the fruit, cheese, and crackers.

It's a good question, and Lily ponders the answer. "I'm not sure," she finally answers. "It just seems like everybody is trying to get something—mostly by pretending they aren't. At least in this group. Other places, they don't lie about it. Maybe I'm just jealous that they want things as simple as admiration or being first or getting lots of stuff."

"Vat do you vant, Lily?" asks Mrs. S, admiring the shine on her good porcelain as she places it, between protective flannel sheets, in the cupboard.

For a second, Lily is tempted to tell Mrs. S about the baby. "Peace," she says on an exhale. "I'm just so tired of the contests and performances and lies."

Mrs. S turns from the cupboard and gazes at Lily with soft eyes. "If you vant peace, you must make peace."

"How?" asks Lily; it's an almost plaintive cry. "How do I make peace when I hear the truth behind everybody's lies?"

"Hear the truth behind your own lies," says Mrs. S. And before Lily can feel the wounding of this statement, "You are a truth teller, Lily. Practice it on yourself. Find friends you can practice with. We all need company. Nobody does it alone."

CHAPTER 11

And that's how the Spectators' Club comes to be.

Even though Lily will inherit the house sale money, she is increasingly, silently frantic about how to make a living, where to live, and what to do to take care of her baby, so when the temp agency calls with another assignment at MoMA, she jumps at the familiarity. It's an action with income attached to it. Maybe the movement will lead to a concrete plan.

She is assigned to the publications' department where she is pleased to re-encounter the women she met in the MoMA cafeteria that horrid day when her boss was fired. Even Lucresse, the older one, is there, directing Lily, wall-eyed Harmony, timid Leslie, strange fat Zelda, and me (Betsy) in the preparations of a promotional mailing. There is something comfortable about this zoo of people who clearly do not fit in at MoMA or probably anywhere. And it is this realization of our common outsider attributes that makes Lily suggest we form a club. She tells us Mrs. S's comments about finding peace by discovering whatever we each may not know about ourselves, and it is such an outsider thought that none of us can figure out a reason to decline the invitation to join this unnamed club.

"The Spectators' Club," says Lily at our first meeting in the parlor of the rooming house, offered by Mrs. S when Lily explained her idea. "What do you think?"

"You're assuming we're going to do this again," says Zelda, considering how many cheese and cracker snacks she can plate without seeming gluttonous. She had hoped there'd be more selection in the free treats and had worn her thrift-store tiered orange and yellow skirt with a twirly ruffle and extra-big pockets for easy food storage.

"It's just an idea," says Lily, blushing.

"A lovely idea," says Lucresse, jumping to her rescue. "You said we'd be observing ourselves and each other, so 'spectators' sounds like a good name. But, tell me, Lily, what exactly—*how* exactly—are we to observe?"

Even though I know the answer to that question, I say nothing, but I watch. As I said, it's what I do.

"And for what purpose?" says Harmony, surprising herself. She's only here because her therapist gave her an assignment to be social and she had no intention of speaking. Like me, she prefers watching. And to deflect, she flips through the pages of the book her therapist loaned her that she brought in case she got bored.

"I don't mean to be rude," says Leslie, before Lily can answer, "but I told my boyfriend I'd be home by three, so I might have to leave early, so just ignore me if I slip out. It's nothing personal. What's that book, Harmony? Leon wants me to read more."

"*Letters to a Young Poet*," says Harmony, tossing it to her. "Take a look."

Lily wills herself to inhale and exhale. "Here's everything I'm hiding. Please observe me while I say it: I'm pregnant and I haven't told anyone. Not even the father, who I want nothing to do with. I didn't wear my diaphragm and I want the baby. I have no idea how I'll take care of it. My family is dead. My mother died two weeks ago."

A stunned silence reverberates around the circle.

"Bummer," says Zelda and we all laugh.

"The reason I'm doing this," continues Lily, as curious about what will come out of her mouth as are Lucresse, Harmony, Leslie, I, and even Zelda—who has stopped eating and is leaning in as if her whole bloated body is ears, "is that Mrs. Schultz, my landlady, is very smart and she said the way to peace is to know the truth under our acts. To find our true nature. You see, everybody is acting all the time, even if they aren't a professional actor like Zelda."

Zelda blushes, and even though she is terrified of sharing any truth—from the fact that she ran away from home at age fourteen and is still a teenager to her completely unfair predicament of being so penniless that she must subsist on shop-"borrowed" packaged goods—she thinks perhaps she is interested in this club of misfits. Perhaps she can help them.

"The problem," continues Lily, "is that it's next to impossible to know what you don't know about yourself, and therefore find peace. So I thought if I could make a club of spectators where we all commit to telling the truth, we could observe each other and help."

Harmony feels a sharp pain behind her eyes and wonders if she has an aneurism.

Lucresse is tired and would love a martini, but she has been sober for twelve years—ever since her husband killed himself, her children announced they wanted nothing to do with her, and she joined A.A. She has had enough hard truth-telling for a lifetime and she is only fifty-five, but these young women are intriguing so she might as well stay and at least listen.

Leslie checks her watch and realizes she forgot to wear it.

"You see," says Lily, with no idea what might follow that clause, but she is blessedly relieved of finding out by the front door nearly exploding off its hinges as the Scully sisters and Shoren brothers return from their double date.

"I just don't understand why," whines Sheba in her hurt, little-girl voice, oblivious to the gathering of women observing her as she races in and searches the sideboard for something. "I mean what's the big deal? I wasn't flirting. He's a commercial contact. It's work. Damn, I could have sworn I left my pictures and resumés in here. Maybe they're in your room, Eddie. Damn." And flipping her hair, she flounces out of the parlor and up the stairs.

"Hi," says Ernie Shoren, blushing at the gathering of women. "Gee, I'm sorry; we didn't mean to—"

"Ernie!" orders Elsie, following Eddie following her sister up the stairs.

"Sorry," says Ernie and sheepishly retreats.

"My point," says Lily, suddenly awash in inexplicable sadness at the sight of the Shorens, but determined to find peace—

"Is everything all right in here?" asks Mrs. Schultz, peeking in from the dining room. "If you need anything, you let me know, Lily. Yah?"

"Thanks, Mrs. Schultz," says Lily and watches Mrs. S withdraw like the tide. "Maybe this was a silly idea."

Leslie says, no, no, it's a fine idea, but she has to meet her boyfriend because it's her brother Peter's death anniversary in Vietnam and her boyfriend is a very observant Jew, a different thing from spectating, and he wants to do *yahrzeit*, whatever that is which she doesn't know because she's assimilated and wasn't raised Jewish, so she must leave this minute, and she races out with Harmony's book.

Zelda determines that this is not a good club for an aspiring professional actress with no funds and a potential avalanche of putrid, possibly felonious, secrets and she says unfortunately she too must skedaddle; she has an audition. But do tell her when the next spectacular meeting is and she shall check her calendar.

And that leaves Lucresse, Harmony, Lily, and me.

Lucresse looks at Lily and sees her lost younger self and feels as if she could cry.

Harmony, despite a budding migraine or aneurism or brain tumor, is intrigued enough to stay and complete the damned therapy assignment, and she makes a note to buy another copy of the Rilke book and hopes that her therapist hadn't marked up the one just filched by Leslie.

And, sensing that this endeavor will be important to me, I say nothing.

"Well," says Lily. And she eats a slice of cheese and a cracker.

CHAPTER 12

We are an unlikely club: beautiful Lucresse with her golden hair and wry smile—a waif even at fifty-five; Harmony, a mixed-race Hillary Clinton look-alike whose wide eyes alternate between drilling their target with laser-like interest and shooting in different directions like hazel pool balls after a break shot; lovely lost Lily; and me. Leslie and Zelda politely declined the invitation to attend our second Spectators' Club meeting.

"It was the silence," says Harmony, looking in all directions, avoiding the rest of us.

Once again, we are in the parlor. It is seven p.m. and dark except for Mrs. Schultz's little glass-shaded side table lamp, which Lily and I barely notice but Lucresse seems fixated on: she could swear it is an original Tiffany—her antique dealer father would have recounted its history in tones simultaneously arrogant and paternal; how she misses that man.

"By the time it happened," continues Harmony, "my mother was completely deaf, but in a way, I liked it even more—no words. Just sitting beside her and watching her sleep. She didn't suffer at the end. It was the silence, you see."

"You shared it," says Lily, matter-of-factly, not even aware that she is jealous. "You shared the silence with your mother." She is so jealous it numbs her, which gives her an odd floaty feeling—not entirely unpleasant. But she is safe in this group of spectators who observe but refuse to speak.

Lily hasn't thought about her mother, let alone her sudden death, in one month. Mrs. S tried to talk to her about it, but Lily isn't interested. She has far more compelling things to attend to—her pregnancy and future and how to negotiate her belly button phobia as it relates to the baby's umbilical cord—and honestly she is annoyed that Harmony has somehow steered the conversation to death. She can't even remember how we got here. Why death? Birth is so much more interesting. And

Lily suddenly remembers that next week is her own birthday. And the realization makes her shudder.

"Are you okay, Lily?" asks Lucresse.

Lily comes to and blushes. "Sorry. I guess I was daydreaming again. It's a bad habit. Sorry."

Nobody speaks for an abnormally long time.

"Sorry to disturb," says Mrs. S from the doorway, holding a platter.

"No, no!" We erupt with the relief of a carful of passengers who have just averted careening off the side of a cliff.

Blushing at her unexpected popularity, Mrs. S offers fresh-baked ginger cookies all 'round and when she starts to exit, assents to our insistence that she sit.

"Zo," she begins, smiling from one of us to the next. "You met at za museum, Lily tells me."

"A horrible place to work," mutters Lucresse between bites. "But it's a job."

"You don't like it?" asks Mrs. S, surprised. "All zat beautiful paintings?"

"But you have to *be* there," says Harmony.

"In an office," says Lily, by way of explanation.

"Politics," adds Lucresse.

"Games," says Harmony.

"There has got to be another way," says Lily.

"Is zere something you all love?" asks Mrs. S conversationally.

The four of us breathe.

"Silence," says Lily finally.

"Yes," mumble Harmony, Lucresse, and I in unison, surprising ourselves.

"Well, zen," says Mrs. S, as though that answers the question. And when the four of us look perplexed, "Instead of our scary selves who don't so much like to talk, let us observe and discover za silence."

And we do.

An hour later, when Mrs. S sighs, we are stunned.

"I've never done that with other people," says Lily softly.

"Vat is zat, dear?" asks Mrs. S, shifting in her rocker and smoothing her skirt.

"Daydreamed."

"Me neither," says Harmony. "I mean seen things in the quiet. While others were there."

"Terrible things," whispers Lucresse, clearly spooked.

"It isn't real," says Lily, shaking herself back to consciousness. "None of it. It's just daydreams."

"Tell me," says Mrs. S, smiling, and although none of them, and certainly I, will ever admit it, we all know that Mrs. S knows exactly what each of us saw. And she is amused!

"It was ridiculous," says Lucresse finally. "My family actually did quite well through the Depression, so I don't know why I should be imagining another one. Perhaps survivor's guilt?" She looks to Mrs. S, imploring. "I've heard that's a real thing. I don't usually worry about finances. I've always had work."

"And I've never lived in a high-rise," offers Harmony, as if this makes sense. "Why on earth should I see them falling?

"Lily?" asks Mrs. S, and Lily shakes her head.

I know she will not answer, but she will never forget what she saw, and feeling a palpable shove in the small of my back, I suddenly find myself leaning forward and expounding on the true nature of time.

Any other place this would be considered a non sequitur, but we are the Spectators' Club, so I don't explain. I just say what I know. Time. Space. Events. Where we go when we daydream. When I finish, shocking myself more than any of the women, I am vibrating and sweating.

"Zo you know this how?" asks Mrs. S pleasantly.

She wants the truth. I lie: "I think I must have read it in a book. Quantum mechanics. I have insomnia and odd taste."

Harmony's eyes have locked into alignment and they are drilling me. "I think I know what you mean: It's like an infinity of boxes, and if you are only focusing on one, you think that's now and that there is a past and a future. But really it's all now—slices of *now* in a box called a lifetime—and there is no series. It just *is*. And once in a while, you can see everything—all possibilities of everything. Or at least more than just the slice of *now* you're in."

Lily is holding her head in her hands. "Like when my mother was telling me about her trip back to Oklahoma, I was *there*. I wasn't remembering it. I wasn't envisioning it because she was remembering it. I was *there. Now*. Feeling what she felt. Like I jumped boxes."

"You can look wherever you choose, whenever you choose," says Mrs. S, smiling. "Ven you speed up to the point of stillness, in the silence, you are everywhere."

"Yes," I say, feeling the vibration subside.

"I have no idea what any of you are talking about," says Lucresse, laughing.

And I think maybe it was all right to have told them.

CHAPTER 13

Although the Spectators' Club dissolves due to loners' disinterest in being a member of any group, Lily, Harmony, Lucresse, and I stay in loose contact, and Mrs. S seems to have taken an interest in Lily that Lily finds peculiar.

"Use me," says Mrs. S. "That is my only prayer."

"I don't understand," says Lily, laboriously stirring the giant soup pot and hoping she didn't just drip sweat into the stew. She doesn't particularly like to cook, but now, three months' pregnant, she knows she must learn to make nutritious and tasty meals, so when Mrs. S offered not only to teach her but to exchange room and board for household services, Lily said yes. It had been increasingly difficult to go to a job, what with morning sickness on top of her general loathing of offices.

"I ask to be useful," explains Mrs. S. "In life."

Lily has never felt remotely useful, so this feels like a useful contemplation and that makes her laugh.

"Zat is funny?" asks Mrs. S. "It is my accent?"

"No, no," says Lily.

"I can't take it!" pronounces Elsie Scully, marching into the kitchen. "My sister is a monster and I'm done. Just done!"

"Ve are making stew," answers Mrs. S. "You vould like to help?"

"No thanks," says Elsie. "I'm nothing to her. Just a target or a convenient dumping ground. It's always been this way. I don't know why I'm still surprised when it happens."

Since neither Mrs. S nor Lily asks what happens, Elsie turns despondent.

"I don't know what I'm doing here," she moans.

"Join the club," mutters Lily, and Elsie looks surprised. "What would make you feel useful?" asks Lily, watching Mrs. S nod in her peripheral vision.

"That's easy," says Elsie, chewing a discarded celery stalk, then using it as a pointing device to indicate Lily's belly.

And that's when Lily has her second technicolor vision—much different from the one that still haunts her from the last Spectators' Cub meeting. She sees a baby goat in a bathroom sink, snow white, soft, and sleepy. In a drowsy trance, it opens and closes its mouth in a suckling motion, then yawns. It's so darling, Lily laughs.

"What's so funny?" snaps Elsie, offended and near tears. "Just because it's traditional, it is not—"

"I'm sorry. I'm so sorry," says Lily. "It wasn't you—"

"Yeah, well—"

"Elsie!" says Mrs. S in such a commanding tone that both young women snap to attention. "You must listen," she says more softly. "You are being given a gift."

Lily, as perplexed now as Elsie, shrinks in confusion. "I'm sorry. It was just a daydream. I didn't mean to—"

"Lily!" commands Mrs. S, and although Lily instantly understands the order, she recoils. "Tell Elsie vat you saw, Lily. And, Elsie, you must listen."

And despite a debilitating blush that starts in Lily's chest and is spreading up her neck, face, and arms, causing her to recoil into a C shape, Lily describes the little goat in the bathroom sink. When she's finished, Elsie has stopped breathing.

"Breathe!" commands Mrs. S and Elsie forces an intake.

"It probably doesn't mean anything," apologizes Lily, dizzy like she is falling backwards through all those time boxes we discussed. If she doesn't sit, she is going to collapse.

"Sit!" commands Mrs. S, and loosening the soup spoon from Lily's white-knuckled grip, she guides her to a kitchen chair.

With a pounding heart and gasping, Elsie makes a hurried breathy excuse about having to go back upstairs to pack, and Lily will never know that she does so to hightail it back to a small town in Southern California where her high school boyfriend is doing an internship for veterinary school. Lily will never hear that Elsie marries him and realizes that she shares his passion for rehabilitating and providing a lifetime sanctuary for baby goats with birth defects, and that she and Roy opt for a farm with these loving and hilarious babies in lieu of the human kind. Lily will never know that in the dark age of Trump and climate change denial, when the wildfires come, Elsie and Roy will die together, trying to save their unusual family—and that's the way they wanted it. She will never hear about all the posthumous awards and tributes and the foundation started in their name that sponsors an international movement to protect helpless creatures in environmental disasters.

"So?" says Mrs. S, hurtling Lily back to "now." "It felt goot, yah?"

"Yah," says Lily, realizing that this bizarre exchange about baby goats reminds her of the open-head feeling during *Bach's Concerto for Two Violins and Orchestra in D Minor*.

"It's love," says Mrs. S.

Lily has never seen daydreaming as a talent, and she wallows in Mrs. S's approval, writing down her "visions" in her diary and discussing them as they prepare dinners. As Mrs. S's house protégé, Lily also discovers a surprising talent for fixing things: broken toilets, flickering lamps, wobbly table legs. She is so good at it that Sheba, who enjoys having her room to herself but misses her sister's handiness, now turns to Lily for quick repairs, and Mrs. S seems tickled when Lily marches into a bathroom with tools and finishes with a flush. Lily is happy to be good at something and derives especial satisfaction from being able to fix something that is broken, but for the life of her, cannot understand the big deal. Anybody can daydream. Anyone can simply stare at a mechanical problem until the connections reveal themselves and therefore the breaks can be found and mended. But Mrs. S piles on the "Goot, goot!" and even seems to think Lily has a future. So, bathed in Mrs. S's delight and with gratitude for her gentle guidance, Lily swan dives into the beginning of what will be an almost half-century of home repairs and a career as a professional psychic.

CHAPTER 14

"This is insane!" yells Lily to no one, and then she writes it in her diary, slams shut the book, and shoves it so hard it slides like a hockey puck under her bed and against the wall. She is lying on her back in the middle of the wood floor of her boarding house bedroom. It's past noon. The Shoren brothers are at work; Elsie Scully is back in California; and Sheba is either waitressing at Schrafft's, at an audition, or having a nooner with a casting director who, years from now when he's a big-time Hollywood producer, will deny ever knowing her when she becomes part of a class-action lawsuit against him for sexual harassment. "I am not going to be a professional fortuneteller!" yells Lily to anybody who might be hanging out in the ether. "I am going to move out of this city and get a regular job someplace safe where my baby can have a normal life." And on the word "life," she curls in pain. "Oh," she moans, rocking and holding her belly. "No!"

And as the cramp spasms through her, she gasps and, panting, crawls for the bathroom. "No, no," she moans between pants. "Please, no, I'll do whatever you want. Just not this." And repressing the overwhelming impulse to push, she barely makes it to the toilet.

"No!" she cries, panting and blowing like an athlete in the final stretch of a sprint, and finally giving in, she pushes and out slides something the size of a small fist, splashing so hard that her bottom is covered with toilet water. "No, no," she keens as she hemorrhages—not because it hurts, because it doesn't; in truth, it is a pleasurable release from the cramps that a minute ago were exploding her insides, and she pushes harder, realizing, when wet hits her bottom, that she will soon overflow the toilet bowl, so without looking—a decision she will regret for the rest of her life—she flushes, and miraculously, it all disappears.

CHAPTER 15

Lily stays in New York City, grateful for the safe home and Mrs. S's certainty that, even if Lily doubts her own visions and hunches and odd ethereal nudges and sense of invisible company, they are something people will pay substantial cash to hear.

"But it's just my imagination," she protests.

"Everything is imagination," counters Mrs. S. "Imagination starts creation. Trust it."

Lily does not trust it. She feels like a fraud when Mrs. S offers her services to members of her Spiritual Discussion Club—free, since Lily is now her apprentice and must accrue as much practice as she can. Mrs. S tells Lily nothing about the first client and she makes sure the woman is a person who was absent for the Thanksgiving meeting when Lily was present. "This is Lily Hogue," she says to the woman as she shows her into the little office off the parlor. "Lily, this is your client." And she backs out smiling.

Frances is a vivacious-looking woman in her late twenties or early thirties, accompanied by her young son. "I'm sorry, but I couldn't find a sitter," she apologizes. "Anthony, why don't you—whoops, no names. I forgot. Don't tell Gretta."

"No problem," says Lily, nodding in a relaxed manner that she hopes looks both seasoned and comforting, following Mrs. S's counsel to convey that she is here to serve.

"Anthony," says the woman, winking at Lily, "you brought your crayons, right? Why don't you do some coloring while Miss Hogue and I have some grown-up talk."

"Yeah, but—" protests the seven-year-old, grabbing his mother's hips from behind and clinging, while drilling Lily with a stare that, were it from an adult, would make her blush.

Weird. A little creepy. But having no experience with small children, Lily assumes she is imagining things, and following Mrs. S's instructions never to fill silence with talk, waits for Frances to settle and come sit beside her on the straight-backed desk chair. Mrs. S insisted Lily use her office because it will be more professional. Lily blushes, nervous.

"Relax," says Frances, smiling easily. "Gretta explained that you are learning. I have absolutely no expectations. I'm happy to be your first guinea pig. How can I help?"

Lily laughs tensely. "Don't tell me anything. Let's see what comes." She takes several measured, deep breaths, just like Mrs. S told her, and closes her eyes as she lets the air out slowly . . . and waits . . . Nothing.

"I'm bored!" yells little Anthony, flinging a crayon across the room and hitting Lily in the forehead.

"Anthony!" snaps Frances, horrified.

"Oh!" gasps Lily, rubbing her forehead.

"I am so sorry," moans Frances, glaring at her son. "Anthony, apologize this minute. What have I told you about frustration?"

And Lily abruptly straightens. "Oh. Oh, my god."

"Did he hurt—"

Lily shushes her with a gesture. "I—please, something's coming. I just need—"

Even though Frances believes none of this and is only here to help Gretta, who used to substitute teach at the school where Frances teaches math, Frances balances on the edge of her chair, suddenly focused on the unspoken question that Gretta advised her to come in with.

"I don't understand this," apologizes Lily.

"Just say it!" commands Frances. And then softens. "I mean, I would be happy to hear whatever you see. Or hear. Or however this works."

Lily is embarrassed. None of this makes sense. The child is seven, for heaven's sake, but Mrs. S told her not to judge, censor, or attempt to translate, and Frances is so needy. "Well, I will just report it."

"Please," Frances nearly squeaks, even though she knows better than to believe an apprentice psychic.

"Your son is appearing to me as a very important man in his forties. Very, very important. Famous even."

Frances claps, unable to suppress her joy. "I knew it! I just knew—" And suddenly she is glad she brought Anthony—not because she couldn't find a sitter, but because of all her many worries about his future, with his many peculiar habits.

Lily holds out a hand for silence, and Frances slaps her own over her mouth and nods, please continue.

"I don't know what he does, but his name is everywhere, and he has something to do with communications. Like pictures or movies, but in miniature," she hesitantly reports.

"A movie star!" gasps Frances.

"But in miniature?" says Lily, certain that she is out of her mind. Whoever heard of miniature movies? "Or maybe it's politics? Or birds?"

Frances looks disconcerted. "Well what is it? Movies, politics, or birds? I've always known he was made for greatness, but birds? Never mind; never mind. Ornithology is fine. As long as it's a good profession. Maybe he's an actor who goes into politics—like Ronald Reagan?" she offers helpfully.

Lily is mystified. "I keep seeing birds and naked people in tiny movies and hearing tweeting. *Tweet-tweet-tweet.* I'm so sorry. I'm really new at this."

Frances huffs, "Naked?" Abruptly she stands, her mouth tightening into a false smile. "Well, I don't suppose there's anything else."

"No," says Lily, dejected. "I'm so sorry."

"At least it didn't cost me anything," quips Frances, attempting to disguise her contempt as humor. "Anthony."

The little boy tosses all his crayons onto the floor, smirks at Lily, and says, "Keep 'em. I got plenty at home."

"Anthony!" demands Frances, and dutifully the child grabs up his crayons and follows his mother out the door.

"So how was it?" bubbles Mrs. S, who has been waiting in the parlor.

In response, Frances gives a sorry shake of her head.

"Stupid broads," groans the boy, marching out to the front door.

"Anthony Weiner!" bellows Frances, "Just wait till your father hears about this!"

That night, Lily has rough dreams: She is pregnant but has no memory of sex. Had she been drugged or raped? Oddly ambivalent, she is grateful for the baby because it makes her normal. Normal women have babies and soon she will become one of them. She hopes it's a girl because she will be more likely to understand her. As the baby grows, so does Lily's sense of purpose, but her mother yells at her, threatening to abandon her if she shames the family with a bastard birth. Her mother is trying to kill the baby. "I'm cutting it out!" she yells, coming after Lily with a birthday cake knife.

"I need you to talk to Leslie!" yells the baby from inside her stomach. And it's a boy.

"What?" says Lily, confused by the competing yellers.

"It's me, Peter!" yells the baby.

"I'm cutting off its peter!" yells Mrs. Hogue, and Lily dives under her bed, stomach first like a baseball player sliding home.

"Tell Leslie I tried, but I gave up!" yells the baby.

"What?" rasps Lily, holding her head in pain and trying to elude her mother.

"You can't have it!" yells Mrs. Hogue, wildly stabbing at Lily under the bed. "You are selfish to want this. It's a mistake!"

"There was no point!" yells the baby.

"Just let me get the point in!" yells Mrs. Hogue, jabbing under the bed with the cake knife which has morphed into a bayonet.

"Tell Leslie: Peter had to give up, but she shouldn't!" yells Peter.

And as Lily slides on her stomach away from the bayonet, her water breaks and the baby escapes, disappearing with a *whoosh* down a drain that suddenly opens under the bed.

Lily wakes sobbing. Oh, how she misses her baby. Peter. His name was Peter. Even though he was a boy, somehow she is certain she would have understood what he needed. She'd have loved and protected him. She'd have— the pain in her heart was like a bayonet stab, right through her, slicing her in half down the gut. She rocks and moans, holding her middle, and when it's over, she sees on her illuminated wind-up alarm clock that belonged to her dead sister whom she never talked to that it's only three a.m.

Who's Peter? she wonders. And who's Leslie?

And then she remembers Leslie Kove from MoMA and her aborted

Spectators' Club and wasn't her brother's name Peter? And she makes a note in her diary: "Call Leslie Kove and tell her Peter gave up but she shouldn't." A note that she will forget for several decades.

The second time Lily wakes, it's to the feeling of a tornado—the same way it is every time Sheba, on the other side of the wall, is preparing for a "this can change my life and make me famous" audition. It's not just the banging of closet doors and thump of discarded shoes against the wall and floor. It is the air itself. As Lily lies in bed, she marvels that this time she not only feels the swirling, but she can see it. It looks like a dust storm if the dust were a white filmy substance, and as it bumps her eyes, she raises a defensive hand—only to quickly realize this energy is unstoppable by mere matter.

"Oh, god," she moans, pulling the covers over her face, and that's when the pounding starts.

"Lily!" hollers Sheba, making the door shake. "Lily, right now! This is urgent. Elsie took my damned shoes! Lily!"

"Coming," moans Lily, grateful for the flimsy sliding lock because it's the only thing keeping Sheba from exploding into the room. "What?" she says, opening the door enough to see Sheba's fully made-up, furious face.

"I need high heels!" she pronounces, pushing past Lily into the room. "Elsie took them and I need them for an audition. At least three inches, preferably more. The ad said 'Tall streetwalker types,' although how they could tell my height on film is dubious. It's a big-studio Hollywood movie. Just put me on a box! I don't suppose you have a cheap gown with a plunging neckline. I won't sweat and I'll have it cleaned. God, the audition's in two hours and I lack basic wardrobe. You don't mind if I just—" and she tears open Lily's armoire and rifles through the dresses and blouses, violently dismissing one after another. "Where are your shoes?" she says, appalled at the two pairs—low-heeled pumps and tennis shoes—and rubber boots. "God, I don't believe this!" And she blows out of the room more violently than she blew in.

Lily rubs her eyes and digs sleep out of the tear ducts. With Sheba out, the Shoren brothers at work, and Mrs. S out of town for the week—one of her unexplained sudden departures, Lily is happy to be in charge of the house. She will finally be able to clean the cat-hair-filled parlor in peace. Unaccountably, she has no cat allergy and she enjoys drawing the lint brush over the furniture, leaving pristine dignity in its wake. She loves dusting all the little sculptures of animals from parts unknown, collected by dead Mr. Schultz before Mrs. S emigrated from Germany. Lily particularly likes the elephants—all sizes, some with sad, knowing eyes that feel eerily real. And Lily doesn't tell anyone, but when she's alone, she whispers to them—nothing specific, just whatever happens to come: "Oh, aren't you beautiful. I'm sorry someone killed you to make this replica out of your tusk. We are a stupid species. You remember everything, don't you? I've heard that. In your DNA, even in this little bit of tusk; there's your whole story. Never forget it. Now let me just get that smudge off. Feel better? Thank you so much for being here, and, again, I'm so sorry."

"The thing is," pronounces Sheba, blowing back into the room, "it's Hollywood."

"I don't wear spike heels," apologizes Lily, amazed that she follows this conversation.

"Purple would be good" says Sheba, undeterred and flouncing onto Lily's unmade bed. "I can wear cashmere unbuttoned. Purple or red would go with it. I wonder if Mrs. S has anything," she adds, hopefully. "I know—you won't go through her things, but *I* could, if you'd just—"

"No!" booms Lily, flinching at her own volume. Then softer, "Besides, I don't even have a key."

Sheba pouts theatrically, then falls back onto Lily's pillow. "Did you know that an orange seed doesn't necessarily grow an orange? It could be a grapefruit or a lemon. That's true for all citrus. Maybe yellow shoes! Do you have any—"

Yellow. Yellow. Yellow shoes? Yellow coat? Something about yellow. Lily's head hurts at the brain scramble of non sequiturs. If only Sheba would leave, but Lily's too polite to ask.

"Oranges are fake fruit," moans Sheba. "Elsie told me. God, I hate her. Where am I going to find shoes? It's not like I have the money—" She peeks at Lily to see if she's worn down yet.

"Sorry," says Lily, deciding to ignore Sheba and privacy and get dressed.

"Elsie says I'm a fake. What do you think about that, Lily?"

Sheba's tone has changed to a timbre Lily has never heard from her. Untheatrical. Human. It's probably another act.

"The ad in *Backstage* said they need 'real people' types—tall prostitute real people. Do you think I'm real, Lily?"

Lily knows exactly what Sheba is, but is too polite to answer.

"Would you do me a favor and just look at the ad? Maybe it doesn't matter how high my heels are. I can be real. Here, I'll read it to you.

> Real women, 18-25, long legs, short skirts, must be comfortable with touching to play streetwalkers in major Hollywood movie. L.A. producer will hold open call, by appointment, at midtown hotel. Mail photo and resume with direct contact info.

What do you think?"

Some man is seeing women in short skirts who don't mind touching in a hotel? Even though she would prefer that Sheba get out of her room, Lily feels compelled to respond. "Did you talk to him to get your appointment?"

Sheba twirls a strand of hennaed hair around her index finger. "No, his assistant called my service; I called him back. Some guy named Max. These big Hollywood types have lackeys for that kind of thing."

Lily tries to sound tired rather than suspicious and certain that Sheba is an idiot. "Is that customary—to have auditions in hotels?"

"I'm not an idiot, you know," snaps Sheba. "Do you think this is a scam?"

"Yes," says Lily. "I think you shouldn't go alone."

And that's how Lily ends up in a urine-soaked vestibule of a hotel on West Forty-second Street next door to a porn bookstore.

"I don't think we should go in there," she says to Sheba.

Ignoring her, Sheba marches to the front desk, announces she is there to see Mr. Seymour Seman—a made-up name worse than Sheba—and before Lily can object, the two of them are riding up to the thirteenth floor in a creaky elevator with battered, graffitied walls and shredded industrial carpet.

"Remember, if he asks, you're just my friend. You came along because we have plans after the audition," commands Sheba.

"I think I can manage that," replies Lily dryly. And, *ding*, the rusty elevator doors scrape open and out they walk into a dimly lit hall so narrow they must travel single file.

Knock-knock.

"Enter! The door is open."

And they are standing in a bedroom. Mr. Seman lounges on his bed in a dingy grey undershirt. Sheba about-faces and Lily has to trot to keep up with her back to the elevator.

"You knew!" huffs Sheba, a few minutes later as they're fast-walking to the bus. "Mrs. Schultz was right. You do have ESP. How did you know? Oh, god, I'm so stupid. I could have been raped. Thank you, Lily. These shoes should be burned. I don't care if they were a hundred dollars. Why the hell did I buy shoes and why can't they make pretty shoes you can walk in? Oh, god, that man was disgusting. I guess I should report him somewhere. There's our bus. I hate these stupid shoes. Although the yellow is rather nice. Maybe a jacket to match them? Run!"

PART II

Recession

Adult cells not only retain a memory of the embryonic and fetal period but also, under certain circumstances, this memory can be recovered.
> —DANA-FARBER CANCER INSTITUTE

CHAPTER 16

Lily never intends to be a charlatan, a fraud, a thief. It's just that people have such high expectations and she doesn't want to disappoint them.

Under Mrs. S's instruction, Lily becomes adept at giving people what they want—making them feel comfortable, understood, safe. From there, it is simple to detect addictions, needs, insecurities, loss. Reading people is reduced to a quick analysis of their "fear of change" correlation to "experience of loss."

"Everybody has lost something," she writes in her diary. "A friend, love, job, security, a fantasy even. The depth of the wound informs how afraid they are of change, which inherently requires the loss of whatever is being changed."

Everybody is addicted to something—excitement, travel, new things, sameness, substances, importance, power, anger, depression, victimhood—and believes that without it, they simply cannot tolerate life. Their fear level determines how confrontational Lily is about naming the addictions and consequently how much she relies on intuitions versus the occasional real psychic vision which does not discriminate about comfort and therefore is as likely to infuriate as comfort them. Generally, she does not even seek anything beyond her sensible intuition, which she is privately loath to attribute to any kind of extra senses. So mostly she just talks, and with Mrs. S's guidance, she effortlessly provides such excellent customer service that, by the time of the great Recession, word-of-mouth has produced a perpetual stream of clients who book months in advance.

To Lily's amazement, following the incident with the pervert on West Forty-second Street, Sheba transforms into her greatest champion. Over the years and with many more off-putting experiences, Sheba becomes a well-known actress—on long-running soaps and on stage. And she founds a nonprofit organization supporting young actresses, advocating for safety and keeping such scrupulous documentation of sexual abuse offenses that the NYPD regularly ignores and the union only pays lip service to that by the time it becomes popular to "out" offenders, she will become even more famous as an expert outraged consultant. But we're getting ahead of ourselves.

Suffice it to say that Sheba refers hundreds, maybe thousands of young performers, who then refer others, to Lily for healing psychic sessions—so many that Lily could survive on the income from them alone. But she doesn't. Hence, when the economy implodes, she has a very comfortable nest egg. Having nothing to do with ESP and everything to do with risk aversion—due to her high-fear-of-change correlation to the wound of the loss of everyone she's ever known—Lily has put most of her declared income into high-interest CDs, a high-interest online checking account with enough for four years' expenses, and a mutual fund that is seventy percent bonds and thirty percent money markets. Not only that, but split between an annuity and an IRA she has the money from the sale of Mrs. S's brownstone and Lucresse's life insurance—the details of which require a bit of backtracking, slowing down your reading speed, and a tolerance for nonlinear storytelling:

When the Spectators' Club disbanded, there remained loose bonds, with Lily at the hub of this odd group of loners. Like a game of telephone, we told one another a bit of news, our whereabouts, etc., and word traveled to Lily.

Zelda McFigg was the first to move out of New York City. For many years none of the other Spectators knew exactly where she was except for a vague sense that it was in New England and she was no longer in show business. However, just before the Recession, she resurfaced briefly—in Beth Israel Hospital.

To explain that, I must note that in 2001, Harmony Rogers died in the World Trade Center attack (finally giving sense to her vision about high-rises falling). All of us learned about the tragedy when her name was listed in the *New York Times* with no details of next of kin. Feeling some guilt, Leslie Kove began looking for records of possible relatives in order to return the filched copy of *Letters to a Young Poet*, which it turned out, was quite enlightening, helping Leslie to value the sometimes overwhelming "questions themselves." When Leslie learned that new 9/11 victim bone fragments had been turned in at Beth Israel Hospital, she went to investigate, leading to the discovery of Zelda McFigg when Leslie, who has never had a sense of direction, took several wrong turns and ended up in the psych ward. "You would hardly have recognized her, she's gotten so fat," Leslie told Lucresse (who had become something of a surrogate mother to all of us), who later told Lily—when Lily accompanied Lucresse to one of her many secret (although who was there to tell?) radiation appointments for her leukemia-induced swollen spleen.

Lucresse was estranged from her three children due to the fact that they still hated her for her many years of alcoholism, before she found "the program" and became sober and so much fun that we Spectators could hardly believe she was ever as insane and abusive as her children remembered. But because they wanted nothing to do with her, Lucresse didn't want to burden them and Lily was happy to be her medical buddy and advocate at the hospital visits.

It was while accompanying Lucresse to one such visit that Lily discovered where Mrs. S disappeared on her mysterious "vacations"—the same cancer wing of New York Hospital where Lucresse eventually died, bequeathing to Lily the life insurance she bought after her vision of a second Depression during our second and final Spectators' Club meeting.

Mrs. S died soon after Lucresse—immediately following the death of her last cat—leaving the brownstone to Lily. Overwhelmed by the administration of owning such a property and on an instinct that had nothing to do with psychic foresight about the housing market implosion and everything to do with grief at the death of two friends, tax forms, and dealing with the NYC Department of Housing, Lily quickly sold the building, instantly becoming a millionaire just before the worst real estate crisis in the history of the world and the Recession of 2008. Which brings us back to the beginning of this chapter and a more linear thread.

You would think people who have lost their 401ks would not include psychic counseling in their budgets, but that is not the case, and by the beginning of 2009, even though she no longer needs the income, Lily cannot bring herself to turn anyone down, and, even though she raises her rates, thinking that will stem the flow, by January her waiting list is filled to the end of May.

In all fairness, Lily is not a complete fraud. Sometimes intuitions and visions come, but more often, with absolutely nothing psychic going on, she practices what Mrs. S called "open talking" where she is also listening—attuned like an antenna to her client's breath and body language responses. She is not seeking to fool anyone. But she knows she is a fraud and rationalizes away any guilt with the fact that she is doing what Mrs. S counseled: Being useful. Helping. Because what she says seems to make people happier.

Therefore, the first conscious fraud shocks her sense of herself as a good person. A good person with no need of money does not research a man she meets in the park. A good person does not lie in wait. A good person does not seduce a client.

CHAPTER 17

It's January 2009, cold, but Lily always finds heat on the heron-shaped rock overlooking Central Park Lake on the small promontory known as Hernshead. Early mornings are usually private with her little dog, Wilma—named after the Flintstone character because she is a strong-willed redhead. Agile at age fifty-eight, Lily bounds up to the edge of the rock and plops down with her long Wellington-booted legs dangling over the side, reflected in the icy water below, along with the tops of Wilma's perky ears—the only part to show when her head is down.

"I should have put your sweater on," Lily mutters to Wilma, who is trembling a little. "Sit on my lap and I'll keep you warm."

But Wilma will have none of that. Although she is small—twelve pounds, a Chihuahua-something mix—she is not a lap dog, and as Lily reaches for her, she bounds off the rock and jumps onto the bench at the base of the small cliff that shields the rock from the more popular Ladies' Pavilion, a shelter that looks as elegant as it sounds, on the other side of the promontory near the public path.

"I guess it is a little cold right next to the water," says Lily, disgruntled, climbing to her feet and moving to the bench. "Is it okay if I sit here too?"

The little dog flops to her stomach, resting her chin on Lily's lap. Lily stares out at the water. Legal things make her sinuses hurt and she doesn't like thinking about money, but now that she has plenty of both, she must: there are two CDs coming due this month plus the fact that she's legally married and suddenly Philip has surfaced asking for a divorce because he wants a new wife. Which reminds Lily of the possibility of trouble since she has been filing taxes as a single person all these years. Add to that the fact that many people prefer to pay in cash for their psychic counseling and god knows how much of that is hidden beneath a floorboard under her bed in her cozy one-bedroom duplex apartment where she sees clients in the parlor—allowing her to deduct one-third of her mortgage—and what if she gets audited? As far as the undeclared cash goes, it was not intentional criminal fraud; it's just that her accounts are online only and she got into the habit of putting it under the floorboard—temporarily, until she could open a neighborhood bank account—almost three years ago, shortly after she sold Mrs. S's brownstone and was so exhausted from the East to West Side move.

"Oh!" says a surprised male voice, startling Lily. "I'm sorry. I didn't expect anybody to be here this early." A short, compact, gray-haired man with thin lips and a hawkish nose stands, awkwardly rocking on his shiny dress shoes, staring at the bench.

Many of the benches in Central Park have rectangular, silver dedication plaques from people who have donated large sums of money for the privilege of memorializing their private sentiments in the public landscape— everything from the "Queen of Mean" Helmsley Hotel diva declaring her $10,000 altruism, to marriage proposals from Davy to Sheila, to nature lovers' devotion to a place, to filial proclamations: "For our hero, R. W. Kensington, Sr., the finest man who ever lived, from his adoring family, Mrs. R. W. Kensingon, R.W. Kensington, Jr., and Richard, Rosamond, and R. W. Kensington, III." Lily has often thought maybe an anonymous bench plaque donation might be a good use of a small bit of her floorboard cash. It suddenly occurs to her that this bench belongs to this prosperous-looking gentleman. "I'm sorry; is this your bench? Your plaque?" she asks.

In answer, the man merely nods and stares.

"We can move," says Lily apologetically, and while the man waits, she picks up Wilma, starts for the promontory rock, then changes her mind and leaves.

"That was unpleasant," she mutters to Wilma.

The next morning, she and Wilma are at Hernshead by seven thirty, certain that they will be able to enjoy their time without intrusion. She starts for the rock, then backtracks, curious about the plaque that belongs to that unpleasant man. She is reading, when she hears his voice.

"Again?" he asks.

Suppressing irritation, she replies pleasantly, "I guess we both like this spot." But this time, she has no intention of surrendering it. She reads aloud: "Jennifer, I cherished my brief time with you. Always and forever, in my death as in life, Roger." The man stares at her, rocking on his dress shoes. "I guess you're not Roger," quips Lily, and she pointedly sits, gesturing that there is plenty of room for the man, if he chooses to share the bench. He doesn't. "That's a different kind of plaque," says Lily, determined to be unperturbed. "Usually living people write them for the dead ones."

The man sits, almost primly, on the far end of the bench. And despite herself, Lily stands and leaves.

A little while later, as she is walking up to Cherry Hill on the other side of the Lake, she laughs, suddenly realizing that she is competitive after all. How ridiculous to get into a territorial battle over a bench. Still, it goads her so much that when she returns home from the morning outing, she types into Google "Roger, Jennifer, Central Park plaque, death" just to see what might come up. And she is astonished when the first listing is a fully produced wedding movie—an ode to the love of Roger and Jennifer, and in the background of the wedding party is the gray-haired man. Not only that, but there are personal details. No last names, but from the chatter and jokes Lily gleans that most of the members of the family are in some kind of business together and they do well enough to own the chunk of beach in the Hamptons that appears as background. The man seems to be a real family man, affectionate with the young couple. "Hey, Milo," he yells, and a joyful, floppy-eared puppy bounds into the wedding party. Feeling like a voyeur, Lily begins to read the comments and soon learns that Roger died three years ago of the same leukemia as Lucresse. Maybe they were at the same hospital at the same time and Lily crossed paths with young Roger. He has such a loving face and he adores his wife. Suddenly Lily feels guilty for being so angry at the gray-haired man. Is he Roger's father? Oh, god, Lily slaps herself and, alarmed, Wilma barks.

The next morning, Lily is expecting the gray-haired man when he arrives. "I'm sorry I was so rude yesterday," she says, starting to move.

"No, no," insists the man. "It was my fault. You have every right to be here. I'm on vacation, which means getting to the office at ten. This is the anniversary of my nephew's death, and I just came early to think. Forgive me."

He is Roger's uncle. Suddenly Lily doesn't feel quite as bad. "All right," she says, sitting down again. "I guess it's okay; you like dogs."

The man shoots her a quizzical look—as Wilma jumps on his leg to be petted.

"They always know," says Lily, who was referring to the dog in the movie, and she quashes a shudder at her almost-gaff.

"I guess so," says the man, scratching Wilma behind an ear. "My nephew had a dog. Milo."

"I'm sorry for your loss," says Lily, cringing at the platitude, but the man doesn't seem to mind.

"I guess it's nice to have a companion in the park," he says wistfully.

"Yes, it is. Why don't you get a dog?"

"Too busy. You have to have time. It's like a child. Not that I ever had time with my children." And he laughs self-deprecatingly.

Lily knows he's seducing her. "I'm sure you could afford a dog walker," she counters.

"You're a smart cookie, aren't you?"

Lily blushes and wishes Wilma would move back to her so she'd have something to hold.

"Don't worry. I like smart cookies. I'm pretty smart myself. Bernard," he says, offering his hand.

"Lily," says Lily, shaking it. He has a nice hand—not too hard, not aggressive, just comfortably there, fully encompassing Lily's.

"So what do you do, Lily, that allows you to spend all your time in the park?" He asks it easily; there is nothing assaultive about this man, and Lily is surprised by his gentleness.

"I wouldn't say I spend *all* my time in the park," she says, laughing. "Just mornings—like you. Wilma and I like this spot."

She notices that Bernard has noticed that she hasn't answered his question about her profession.

"I don't do anything very exciting. I'm kind of a counselor. How about you?"

"Oh, that does sound interesting," he replies. "A lot more interesting than working with numbers all day. I'm very boring." And then after a reflective pause, "Sometimes I think I could use some counseling. What sort of things do you do?"

"Nothing that impressive. I'm not licensed or anything."

Bernard waits. Lily knows what lies down this road and she makes a split-second decision to explore the mess.

"I'm a psychic counselor. I don't even know if I believe in it." She laughs flippantly. Bernard does not laugh; he looks very serious.

"Why do you do that?"

"What?" says Lily, knowing exactly what he's talking about.

"You know exactly what I'm talking about."

"I don't know. I suppose I expect people to roll their eyes, so I do it first."

"What am I thinking now?" says Bernard, smiling.

What the hell, thinks Lily, and she goes for it. "I don't counsel people I know."

"But you don't know me," answers Bernard pleasantly. "I'm sure you're expensive and booked well in advance. How about I pay twice your normal fee and you see me on Friday?"

This is insane, thinks Lily, as she washes individual leaves of Mrs. S's ficus tree and brushes the dust off Lucresse's African violets, then vacuums her parlor a second time early Friday morning. She never gets nervous before appointments. Her clients are all basket cases and something about that renders Lily rather Zen. Everybody always remarks on her goddamn calming presence and healing demeanor! As she vigorously polishes the scarred coffee table for the third time, she thinks maybe she can just tell him that she watched the YouTube video. No, no, never! Only a stalker would do such a thing. There is no way to tell him the truth, and there is no way to erase what she saw—a family man, beach house, wealth, tension between him and his sons, his overseer attitude about everything, and his incredibly attractive unflappable confidence. She cannot unsort this and do an untainted reading. But wait! Maybe she'll actually get a vision that will surprise her. The fact that she hasn't had one in years makes her laugh. She'll just tell him this was a mistake, ask him specifically what he wants help with, and say she'll try her best, and if nothing useful comes, she will not take his money. Not that he cares. The man reeks of money. Oh, god, if only Lucresse or Mrs. S were alive!

Lily willfully stops cleaning and breathes in the room. There is some comfort in being surrounded by Lucresse's and Mrs. S's things. Although Lily's home is a first and second-floor duplex on West Seventy-fourth Street, two blocks from Central Park, it is a quarter the size of Mrs. S's and Lily had to be selective in the furnishings she kept. Modeling the first-floor parlor, formerly a studio apartment, after Mrs. S's, Lily uses it for sessions. The room is appointed with a fat, squishy burgundy sofa with rolled arms, comfortable squishy, dark-blue side chairs, and an old-world beechwood and glass display cabinet filled with Mrs. S's ivory elephants and other treasures. This room, grounded on Mrs. S's warm burgundy Persian rug, makes clients instantly comfortable.

Most of Lucresse's things—paintings—are upstairs in Lily's private living quarters—a bedroom, living room, office, and full bathroom. Lucresse loved her art, and Lily loves it because it reminds her of their friendship. Her favorite piece is an oil painting of three women sitting around a table laughing. The younger one, a yellow-haired beauty with a long neck, has her head flung back and mouth open while two grinning older women point at her. Lily sees it as a portrait of herself with Lucresse and Mrs. S in their last good time in the hospital.

When Lucresse first asked Lily if she would accompany her to doctors' appointments, Lily was surprised. Other than the lunches at MoMA, the two Spectators' Club meetings, and a few phone calls, they didn't know each other that well. Lily liked Lucresse and assumed it was mutual, but there was nothing intimate enough to merit becoming a medical buddy and hospital advocate. And perhaps because it was awkward in an exam room helping Lucresse disrobe for radiation, or asking the doctor questions Lucresse had forgotten to ask, or reminding Lucresse of the answers she couldn't remember hearing following the zapping, Lily feigned nonjudgmental competence. She feigned it so well that by the time she and Lucresse had their run-in with Mrs. S in the radiation department of New York Hospital, Lily had actually achieved nonjudgmental competence, real compassion, and the kind of easy relationship she never could have had with her mother.

"You shouldn't come here alone," Lucresse advised Mrs. S when they had discovered her in the waiting room of radiology.

"I zuppose," said Mrs. S, emphasizing her accent. "But I'm an old woman, all alone, who vould come mid me?" She shot a wicked smile from Lily to Lucresse so that all three of them laughed, and from that moment on, radiation appointments were synchronized so that Lily could accompany both women.

Applying to this advocacy/buddy job all of her conscientious office skills, Lily made sure they were thirty minutes early, giving her time to check in both women and request that they be placed in adjacent exam rooms so that she could gallop from one to the other, aiding them with their clothes and the ridiculous hospital gowns that, if not adjusted just so, exposed one's privates. Her top priority was ensuring maximum modesty for both women in this potentially embarrassing venue where the receptionist couldn't interrupt her phone conversations to keep track of who was where, and technicians slammed in and out of rooms, leaving doors open and buttocks exposed, and she was deadly serious as she demanded that they wait for her assistance so that they could change with the door closed. To say she was shocked the day that Lucresse and Mrs. S took control of the situation is an understatement.

"Wait for me!" Lily ordered Lucresse, after she was seated on the exam table. "I'll be right back."

And she literally ran across the hall to Mrs. S.

"Wait for me!" she commanded after Mrs. S had handed Lily her coat and was seated on her table.

And then Lily galloped back to Lucresse—who, in one rehearsed movement, had ripped off her dress and underwear so that she greeted Lily stark naked with her six-month-pregnant–size spleen and a demonic smile. "What are you doing?!" screamed Lily.

Lucresse laughed so hard the exam table squeaked.

"Lily!" hollered Mrs. S from across the hall. "Come now! Emergency!"

"For god's sake put on a robe!" hissed Lily, running back across the hall—to find Mrs. S exposing her one-breasted self, wearing only a coy smile.

"You're both wretched old women!" boomed Lily so loud that the receptionist stopped chatting and an orderly dropped his tray.

That was the day the friendships were cemented. And after that, it was a game to see if Lily could keep the women clothed with the doors closed. Sometimes she could, sometimes not. And all it took was the "look"—the coy or demonic smile—to send all three of the women into paroxysms of laughter.

Imagine, Lily thinks now, looking around her parlor missing them. Imagine turning brutal radiation into fun. And she imagines she can hear them both laughing. Oh how she misses the laughs.

Bernard is late for the appointment, and Lily's nervousness turns to irritation. After half an hour, she phones the contact number he gave her and it goes straight to voicemail. "That's it!" she says to Wilma. "I am so sick of these people and I will not sit around waiting." At a loss for what to do instead, she grabs Wilma's leash even though she already gave her an extra-long walk this morning and heads for her coat and the door—just as the intercom buzzes.

Lily opens her door to check, and there is Bernard smiling sheepishly and waving through the glass building door. Relieved that she doesn't have to hate him, she buzzes him in.

"I apologize," he huffs, carrying a large brown-paper-covered parcel. "I had an irresistible impulse—I'm sure you understand—and I took a side trip on the way. Here," he says, holding the parcel out. "Kind of heavy. Maybe I should bring it— Oh, this is lovely, Lily. That's a cherrywood entry hutch!" he says, shooting an appraiser's vertical scan at Mrs. S's mirrored hall tree. And then moving into the parlor, "What a comfortable room! I'll just put this down here. Tell me where to sit. You're in charge. I put myself in your capable intuitive hands. Again, I apologize for my lateness. But being so intuitive, you probably knew exactly what I was doing. Do me a favor and act surprised just to humor me."

Despite herself, Lily laughs and forgives him his lateness.

"Should I open this now, or after your session?" she asks, almost shyly.

Bernard makes a display of shrugging that the decision is hers.

Lily carefully peels back the tape from one end of the parcel, then peeking inside, gasps and rips.

"It reminds me of you," says Bernard, smiling.

Lily is having trouble breathing. "What made you think that?" she almost whispers, staring at the full-size framed print of Chagall's "The Birthday."

"Maybe I'm a little bit psychic myself. My clients have always thought so. I'm very good with money."

He smiles so charmingly for a man with almost no lips. "Listen, Bernard—"

"I won't hear of it. It popped into my head and yelled, 'Li-ly!' You must keep it. It's only a reproduction. Bogus. A fraud. A fake!" He grins slyly.

Suddenly noticing that she forgot to clean the display cabinet glass, Lily feels off balance, but she learned long ago to accept that. Sometimes when the rare visions do come, they are preceded by a vertiginous airiness, as if the floor is rocking and her head is being sucked up from the crown. "All right. Well, thank you, Bernard. Shall we get started? I sit here," she says, settling into her blue chair. "You can take the other chair or the couch—wherever you feel most comfortable."

"It's a very romantic painting, don't you think?" says Bernard, assessing the furniture, then choosing the couch. "Don't worry. I'm a happily married man. I'm not going to try anything."

Lily blushes and covers her sudden wash of relief and disappointment by rubbing her hands together and breathing deeply several times, as if preparing for psychic visions. Then she closes her eyes. And waits. And opens them. Bernard is smiling pleasantly. "Listen, Bernard, this is awkward, but being psychic or having visions or knowings or whatever you want to call them, it's really not in my control—"

"I know," he answers simply. "I've been around the block, Lily. Just talk. Say whatever comes to you. I'm curious; that's all. I don't want anything from you."

And his last sentence hits like a wave of comfort—warm, soft, safe like a big teddy-bear, man-size hug. Lily collapses into a slump.

"Bad posture feels so good, doesn't it?" sighs Bernard, seeming to enjoy whatever Lily presents—seeming to enjoy *Lily*. The real Lily. Lily doesn't know what to make of this, but it feels good. She hasn't felt this good since the radiation visits at New York Hospital.

"Lily, no," whispers a voice that isn't there. And Lily shakes her head dismissively. "No," it insists, and if she didn't know better—that she almost never experiences audio clairvoyance, only occasional images, however fleeting—she would swear it is dead Harmony from the Spectators' Club. But that is ridiculous. They weren't even close.

"What is it?" asks Bernard. "Tell me."

Lily shakes her head again and then looks at him. He is a nice man. She is going to tell him the truth. "The truth is, Bernard, I'm mostly a fraud."

"Oh, Lily," groans Bernard.

"No, please, let me finish. I promise I'll give you any intuitions I have and you can decide if they're helpful, but I'm not going to take your money. I watched a YouTube video about you."

Bernard's smooth pie face cracks into a slow smile that pouches out his cheeks as it spreads to crinkles around his eyes. And he laughs. He doubles over, slaps his thighs, and howls.

"You think this is funny?" gasps Lily.

"The wedding video!" coughs Bernard between laughs. "You looked up the bench plaque and found the wedding video!"

"Yes," says Lily, perturbed. "And you're not mad? You think that's funny?" Lily isn't sure, but she could swear she detects relief in his laughter. Why?

Bernard laughs till he can't breathe. Lily watches. And slowly she stops caring. She doesn't care that what she's doing—what she does—is ridiculous; that most of the people who come to her don't want to hear that it's ridiculous; that, except for Wilma, she hasn't had a really good friend since Lucresse and Mrs. S died; that once Wilma dies, she will most likely off herself; that she has never had any idea what she's doing here; that even though she once felt bliss listening to a piece of music, she long ago gave up chasing that feeling, and even if it came again—perhaps, after Bernard leaves and she hangs the Chagall, she will stare at it for several hours—it wouldn't change the fact that she's done. Done being a person. Done living. Done serving human time. Done.

"It's not that I've never experienced psychic knowledge. It used to happen a lot more, in the beginning. I worked as a temp at the Museum of

Modern Art, which is when I fell in love with that picture you brought me. You're probably not surprised. I used to have intuitions there—like I was sitting in on somebody else's life, something I had no business knowing when I was in the first miserable little office they put me in. And years later, I found out it was converted into a bedroom by Nelson Rockefeller when he used the brownstone as a private residence and— Well, you know the story. Everybody does. And once I even started a club of psychics—my landlady suggested finding community, and she was a psychic. Not like me, but the real thing. And she thought I could do it too, so I formed a club with a bunch of people and we sat around and had visions and I saw the most horrendous— Well, who knows. It's never happened. But Harmony saw 9/11—she was a member of the club—and she couldn't do anything about it and even died in it. So what's the point? Maybe that's why I stopped having the visions. What's the point of knowing something bad is going to happen when you can't do anything to stop it? And all these people, they pay me and I take their money, and I don't even need it anymore; I have all the money a person could want, more than I can ever spend, yet they keep coming. What the hell am I doing? Excuse my French. Thank you for the print. I have no idea what I'm talking about or why you are still sitting here listening."

Bernard looks at her with the soft, sad eyes of an old soldier remembering a battlefield.

"What do you want, Lily?" he finally asks.

He looks so tired that it makes Lily tired too, and even more relaxed, even less caring. What's the point of hiding anything? So she answers. "If I knew the answer to that, don't you think I'd do it, or buy it?"

"Let me put it another way," he says, sounding like a patient grandpa instead of a high-flying financier who has a chauffeur waiting to take him to a day full of appointments and important phone calls. "What are you afraid of?"

Lily thinks. And shrugs.

"Mind if I take a guess?" he asks.

Again, she shrugs.

"You work as a psychic. You hold people. You tell them things that give them hope, that make them feel better, yes?"

She nods.

"In a way, you may even be a container for them to fall into so that they can face shame, remorse, mortification of being jealous and cruel, incapable of love, users, abusers. Did you ever read *The Catcher in the Rye*? A fine book. I met Salinger once. May have even done some business for him, but don't tell anyone. Like your work, mine is absolutely confidential. I'm only mentioning it because you promise confidentiality too. Am I right?"

Lily nods, mesmerized.

"Holden Caulfield wanted to be a catcher in the rye; but I think you think it would be even better to be a holder, a container, so nobody would even approach the jumping off. True?"

Lily nods. Who is this man who knows everything?

"And I have a sneaking suspicion you are tired from all this helping and containing, and you're afraid to admit that maybe you need somebody to do those things for you."

Lily can't speak.

"Now I'm going to tell you some things, and if any of this makes you uncomfortable, just say so. As I said, I don't want anything. I'm just offering. My work is, in many ways, similar to yours. I'm a very good container."

Again, Lily nods.

"I mentioned that I work in finance. Well, actually what I do is make a lot of money for a lot of very wealthy people. I do that many ways. And sometimes I set up ways for them to do good philanthropic work. You said you are comfortable, so maybe that would interest you. Putting your income to work for good causes. Perhaps that's the purpose you're longing for. Perhaps you just need somebody to fall into who can make that happen."

Lily may be lonely, purposeless, and liminally suicidal, but she is not a fool. Nor does Bernard want her to be. He gives her plenty of references and she also checks with the lawyer who handled Mrs. S's building sale. To say he is impressed is an understatement.

"Do you have any idea who this man is?" he almost gasps. "He started NASDAQ. The guy is a legend!"

Lily cannot believe her luck. Not only does Bernard take over all of her investments, consolidating them into his elite high-paying fund, but he assures her that he will handle setting up a foundation fund for philanthropy and have one of his associates deal with her soon-to-be ex-husband, Philip.

Eleven months later, when the infamous Bernie Madoff scandal breaks, Lily believes she has found her purpose, is unmarried, and has happily contributed to child welfare organizations, women's shelters, animal protection societies, conservation, and anybody else who has struck her as deserving, only to find out nobody has received any money from her and all she has left is her fortunately massive checking account and the floorboard cash. Not only that, but Philip, having learned about her wealth when she is publicly listed as one of Madoff's victims, is asking for a ridiculous payment to compensate him for the fraction of a year his father supported Lily in the horrible West Eighty-first Street hovel with street furniture as well as the "pain and suffering" of estrangement when she decided to "walk out on him."

There is a pleasantness to the collapse and exhaustion after passing through the crucible of failure. Oddly, Lily feels this after having been in and then dropped by Bernie's steady, scamming arms. He was easy to talk to. She thought she was seducing him, but learning that it was a double cross is strangely comforting; she can now see herself as a good person who was victimized. No responsibility. The fact that he's a fraud too seems karmically just. He made people comfortable with his good instincts the same way she did. She retired from her psychic work shortly after becoming a philanthropist. Bernie gave her license not to act by promising to contain all her needs and do everything. At least she still owns her apartment.

PART III

The Late Years

Researchers can only speculate about why adult cells preserve these molecular memories. One possibility is that they're simply relics of an earlier stage of cells' lineage— fossils of their course of development. Another is that cells may need to summon these memories—to bring them to life, in effect—in order to generate fresh tissue to repair damage. "If the body needs to regenerate tissue that is damaged, it may be necessary for cells within that tissue to replay what happened in the embryo," Shivdasani states.

—DANA-FARBER CANCER INSTITUTE

CHAPTER 18

The fall of Madoff and the loss of her wealth make Lily giddy—the kind of bubble-headedness one might feel after falling off a mountain only to discover no broken bones and a curious new terrain—resulting in an even curiouser thing: Lily becomes interested in the world around her and she begins to smell it with a suddenly supersensitive olfactory system.

The year she retires from being a psychic, Lily does not go to the theater, travel, or have any of the adventures she'd contemplated. Nor does she attend the benefits of the beneficiaries of her intended philanthropy, whose mailing lists she is on from "liking" their Facebook pages. Instead, she goes on walks with Wilma and explores life by reading books. Many books. As part of her new reading habit and in an attempt to be social, she joins Goodreads, a popular book readers' site, and like many discreet members, she does so under a pseudonym: Happy Yellow Pumpkin. No reason other than it makes her smile. For a profile photo, she uses a demonic looking jack-o'-lantern with a three-tooth grin wearing a floppy yellow hat and a yellow parka. And to mitigate the effects of sedentary reading, she begins working out to Kathy Smith DVDs.

By the spring of 2010, she has well-developed deltoids and has read thirty-three books—she keeps a list; she has joined and left two book clubs (she didn't like the book choices or the smell of the people), one beginning knitting club (she discovered she has no interest in making things out of wool), one exercise class (again, the smell problem, and Kathy Smith is always there, frozen at age twenty-five and friendly), and several early-morning dog play groups because Lily is bored by the chatter and prefers silent walks with Wilma.

Does attachment to other people require a love of small talk? she wonders. What's a girl with an attachment disorder, hypersensitive olfactories, and a low threshold for meaningless talk to do? She laughs and then considers accepting some psychic appointments—she still gets calls—

but the thought implodes in an inner collapse. Although her detachment makes her good at the work, the work itself is dry. Bone dry. Where is the juice? she wonders. Why is everyone trying so hard? What do they want? Why don't I want anything? Other than loving Wilma, why am I here? Certainly there is something wrong with me, but I don't want to be addicted to people or things or anything. Is there purpose without attachment? Is the world screwed up or am I?

Lily does not like thinking about money, but three months into her second year without income, with early Social Security three years off, even though there is plenty left in her checking account and a fortune under the floor, she feels that worrying is the responsible thing to do. She and Wilma have just started across Central Park's famous Bow Bridge on the way into New York City's woodlands, known as the Ramble, when she is enveloped by one of the many tour groups that travel in hoards, led by guides with red umbrellas. Picking up Wilma and juggling her with the book she's reading, Erik Larson's history of the Chicago World's Fair, *The Devil in the White City*, Lily tries to flatten herself against the cast-iron railing. She hates these crowds but has learned it's best to make herself as small as possible and wait for them to recede like the technology-obsessed human cesspool that they are. Being invisible in front of such people is effortless, as they walk without seeing anything that is not in focus through their cell phone cameras. To be large and visible is to be trampled without apology.

"This is the famous Bow Bridge connecting Cherry Hill to the Ramble, thirty-six acres of woodland. The bridge, designed by Calvert Vaux in the mid-nineteenth century, may look familiar because it has been used in countless movies, such as *Manhattan*, *The Way We Were*, and too many commercials to name," announces the guide, twirling his umbrella and talking much louder than necessary since he is using a megaphone. "Vaux was partners with renowned landscape architect Frederick Law Olmstead and together they worked on this park between 1858 and 1876."

There is the sound of cawing and a tussle near the back of the crowd. Like a good stage performer, the guide waits it out. "Everybody okay back there?"

In response, a crooked old man with a Santa Claus beard, dressed in a gray wool suit with an out-of-season, out-of-style brown overcoat, waves his cane in the air as if to bat something away. "Damned crows," he says to no one.

"All right then," continues the guide. "You should know that this entire park—every rock, tree, and water body—is a manmade creation. Olmstead was something of a control freak and insisted that his original design be sacrosanct. I'm sure he would be pleased about the eight urns you see on either side," and he points with his umbrella like a flight attendant indicating the exits. "They are a recent restoration since the originals went missing more than eighty years ago."

"It's about time!" huffs the crooked old man with the beard. "It took a lot of juice to come up with that plan!" Then in an odd, bird-like way, he rotates his head to make sudden and direct eye contact with Lily, who is flattened against the rail, almost in the bridge's gutter, clutching Wilma. He winks.

Lily waits for the guide to finish and the crowd to recede back to the mainland. Relieved when they are gone, she puts down Wilma and the two of them continue across the bridge and up the hill through the woods to the Ramble hut, now known on its official 1982 restoration plaque as the Rustic Shelter. The hut is an open-walled house of rough-hewn tree limbs where homeless people sometimes camp and gay men have sex. Lily prays it will be empty and odorless. She wants to sit by herself on the worn slab benches with her boots in the dirt and read her book while Wilma does whatever she wants to do.

Yes! It's empty. And even though it stinks of misuse, she sits and opens her library book. Lily doesn't read much history, but a new book club she's decided to try—third time might be kismet—has picked *The Devil in the White City* as its April read. It's not bad—the story of a psychopathic killer who possesses his victims by murdering them, interwoven with the history of the Chicago World's Fair. Since she spends so much time in a park designed by Frederick Law Olmstead, who also designed the fairgrounds, she is curious about the man. Was he a control freak? She accepts that the park is a totally manmade landscape, but how arrogant to take credit for every bird, squirrel, and raccoon, and what about all the little plants that pop through the asphalt? Was the terrain not a partnership of man and nature? Or a battle—the way the Central Park

Conservancy, a privately funded elite garden club, treats it, destroying thriving barberry bushes and the ancient weeping willow that used to drape over the edge of the Lake because their membership suddenly decided that they were destroying pleasing sightlines!

Caw-caw!

That damned crow again.

As Wilma noses around the perimeter of the hut, Lily checks to see that there are no condoms or other dangerous-if-swallowed debris, and satisfied that the environment is safe, she opens her book:

> Olmstead himself had grown increasingly susceptible to
> illness. He was sixty-eight years old and partly lame from
> a decades-old carriage accident that left one leg an inch
> shorter than the other. . .

She turns the page to discover that somebody has left a computer print-out of a John Singer Sargent painting of Olmstead, dated 1895. Lily does a double take. He has a Santa Claus beard, is dressed in a gray wool suit with a brown overcoat, and he is leaning on a cane.

This isn't possible. Lily shakes her head. This is the man she just saw—

"So what are you going to do?" asks a voice behind her.

Lily whirls around. Nobody.

"Long time, no see," says the voice, and Wilma growls.

"Holy shit!" gasps Lily, seeing who it is—Harmony Rogers from the Spectators' Club, now standing in front of her, just as real as Olmstead a few minutes ago.

"Wilma, hush. I'm sorry," she says, grabbing for her harness. "What are you doing here? I mean how—"

"Glad to see you too," says Harmony. "Small world. Don't worry about Wilma. I like dogs." She sits with a squishing sound. She takes up half the bench. Apparently you can gain weight after death.

"I don't understand," gasps Lily.

"I'm still a spectator," says Harmony, enjoying Lily's confusion. "I tried to warn you about Bernie, but you wouldn't listen. So this time, I decided to make an appearance."

"This is insane," says Lily.

"Probably," agrees Harmony. "But you've been thinking about offing yourself. Pretty insane if you ask me."

"I—. It's none of your business. I'm not going to do it. I've just had a lot on my mind. I lost a lot of my money."

"So make some more," quips Harmony. "You never had a problem with that before."

"I can't do it," mutters Lily. "It's bogus."

"Is seeing me bogus?"

"Maybe. Maybe I'm insane."

"Well, be that as it may, you're seeing me, right?"

"Seems so."

"So tell me what's going on."

And simply because she cannot think of a reason not to, Lily tells Harmony about her lack of juice.

"Juice is easy," says Harmony, almost bored. "Orgasms. Next problem?"

Lily scoffs. "Right. I don't want to be with anybody. I know that probably sounds weird, but—"

"Not at all," quips Harmony. "Masturbation. Try it. There's your juice.

Next problem?"

Lily can't believe she is taking this conversation seriously, but Wilma has stopped growling and she always found Harmony mysteriously interesting. And how often do you get to talk to a ghost?

"I don't know why I'm here," she says. "I don't know why I'm me, able to see you. I don't know why I know things when I know them—you knew about 9/11 and you still got killed."

Harmony shrugs.

"So when my money runs out and Wilma's gone . . ."

"Why don't you write about it? Something other than that trunk full of diaries might be a good exercise."

Lily gasps.

"Maybe telling a story will help you find out why you're here," suggests Harmony helpfully. "You know I used to be a magazine editor—of sorts; not worth going into; asshole boss. The point is, you have good stories, and you like reading them. So write them. When you write, you learn. When you write, you can have whatever you want—whatever you write. Maybe you could make some money that way."

And because Lily has never worked in publishing, she does not laugh. Instead she asks, "How would I do that? I've never written anything."

"Do you remember that woman, Betsy, from our group? She's a book editor. Why don't you call her?" And *poof* she is gone and the damned cawing starts again.

Within the space of two weeks, Wilma stops being able to jump up on the couch and drags on the way to the park. Her face turned white last year, but she remained so puppy-like that Lily had convinced herself that she would never get elderly. The new slowness feels like a boulder-size weight on Lily's heart. She isn't ready. She doesn't have anything she wants to do, but still, she isn't ready for old age. When Wilma sits after only half a block's walk, refusing to go to the park at all, Lily begins to cry. It starts as wordless tears, but by the time she's opening the apartment door, it is full-fledged weeping, the kind of grief she knows she should have felt when her mother died. She cries because her only friend is going to leave her, because she lost so much money and Bernie Madoff, who promised to be a container, was a psychopath and she doesn't believe in psychic advising but that's all she's done so she isn't eligible for unemployment insurance. She cries because a professor at the University of Alabama went on a shooting rampage—killing three, wounding three—because he was denied tenure, and she cries because some human herd leaders said it was okay and therefore millions of women of all shapes and sizes are wearing black tights called leggings that, when stretched over behinds, become so sheer that either knowingly or unknowingly women are walking around with fully visible butt cheeks. Lily cries and cries and she keeps crying because she doesn't know how to stop. And then she makes a list. She hasn't done that since her marriage, but it worked then, so why not now?

What do I want? she writes in her newest diary, feeling sheepish and wondering if Harmony is watching from the ether.

To have Wilma forever.

What do I want that I don't have that I could have?
Juice.

What, in everyday life, do I like?
Wilma.

What is it about Wilma?
Juice. The juice of love. The juice of life.

And then remembering Harmony's advice, she goes into the bedroom, slides off her blue jeans and underwear, and begins to rub.

"This is absurd," she says out loud. "I don't even believe in ghosts. Or if I do, that they'd come and tell me to masturbate. And I'm not even horny."

"It's irrelevant," says Harmony's voice inside Lily's head. She sounds like she is yawning under water.

So Lily continues. Since menopause, she is dry, so she spits on her fingers. She is surprised when the first sensations start, and she remembers she used to like this. After their wedding night, things with Philip actually got pretty good—not that she ever loved him, but they did manage to give each other pleasure.

She puts a fist under her low back to tilt it up so her pelvis falls into an open and almost helpless yawn. Surrender. Yes, she remembers. At the first tickle of deep pleasure her breath comes in pants, and she bears down harder, her hand knowing just how to press, when to release and let it throb, when to resume. How on earth could a man be expected to be in such sync? And then it comes—the contraction of energy in her uterus, tighter, tighter, and explosion sending tingles through her face as hot electricity floods her. Her neck arches and she finds she is biting her lower lip. Again. And again. Gasping, she lies back and feels her vagina throb on its own. Then just after a plateau, she cups it and one press and again, explosion. Why has she ignored herself all these years? Wilma flees the bed to hide underneath. "Everything's fine, sweetheart." Lily gasps. "Don't be scared."

Her gynecologist said her uterus is shrunken to the size of a walnut, but she could swear it is huge and pulsating—blissfully raw and almost painful. What if I just press, she thinks, four fingers around her mound and the thumb on—in—the uterus point, my god, inside, she's inside, she presses and her whole body explodes.

And when it's all over, she is full. This is juice.

She slides into her underwear and jeans and hurries to the bathroom, rinses her hand, then out to the desk in her living room, boots up her laptop, and opens a new Word document. She will write a book, a bestseller maybe, and all those book lovers on Goodreads will read it and have arguments about it, and maybe book clubs will want it, and certainly that should bring in enough money to preserve her nest egg until Social Security.

She looks at the blank page and wonders what to write.

Two hours later, she insists that Wilma go for a real walk. She has no idea where Betsy is—she must have moved since their Spectators meeting decades ago—but perhaps she will try the last number she has for her and try to get some advice.

CHAPTER 19

Lily has been reading Ian McEwan books. The last one had a lot of sex and masturbation. Could she be daring enough to start a book—a novel, because nobody would believe the truth—with an orgasm? Readers like to be hooked from the first sentence. Certainly an orgasm—an explosion—would be a good start. She could describe it using many adjectives just like McEwan, who writes scintillating narrative. She knows she has a thesaurus somewhere. She could write a story about a woman who is very good at home repairs—toilet fixing and such—but she spends most of her life watching other people, then realizes that even though she can rewire a lamp, she doesn't know herself when she suddenly discovers that her body's wiring allows her to have an orgasm merely by pressing her thumb into the center of her pelvis. But then what does the woman do? What does she do for a living? Perhaps, like Lily, she works as a psychic. That could be interesting to people. Or perhaps the orgasm is the end of the story.

After several days of feeling like she is falling backwards through a vacuum of empty pondering, interrupted by innumerable and unrelenting intercom buzzes from Amazon Prime, Lily decides that, except for the masturbation part, Harmony's suggestions were moronic, and she has no interest in writing a book, but she is fed up with acting as a container for her neighbors' parcels, so she must express that:

To All Delivery Persons Attempting to Deliver Packages for My Neighbors

Yes, I work at home, but kindly do not ring my buzzer if your package is not for me!

Why?

1. Because I am 1A/2A.

2. Because I am not my neighbors.

3. Because, just like you, I work. I would dearly like you to understand the meaning of that statement, as clearly

my neighbors have not considered that their nightly online shopping habits require another person who is working to stop what she is doing in order to function as their concierge!

Therefore, even if you lean on my buzzer for one full minute—which several of you seem to believe will entice me, I will not:

1. excuse myself from my business call,

2. get out of the shower or off the toilet,

3. put down the book I'm engrossed in,

4. abort my daily full-body video workout mid–sit-up which is the only thing that ensures a modicum of sanity during the hours of solitude, or

5. lose my inspiration and destroy the creative flow of whatever I am laboring at.

In short, I would like to assure you that no matter how many times or how long you buzz, I prefer to sit here with my shattered concentration, ignoring you by tearing my hair out and cursing my neighbors—who, by the way, I am now certain are hoarders, so it might behoove all of us to avoid enabling them—than answer the intercom.

Furthermore:

Since it seems to have become common knowledge among the delivery community that I work at home, although I do admire imagination, I really do not appreciate your subterfuge:

1. Replying to my request for the name of the package's recipient by saying it is for me, and then feigning confusion when I appear to sign for it.

2. Leaving the package that you have said is for me outside the brownstone's front door in the open air and running away before I arrive so that I am now responsible for the package's secure delivery and I cannot give you a dirty look.

3. Practicing relentless syncopated buzzer pressing and

other inventively annoying patterns even though, more
than once, you have promised to never ever buzz me again
for a package for my neighbors, and yet you know I am
here—because you have peeked in my front window and
detected light—occupied with something that is as important to me—or maybe not, but really, does it matter?—as
package delivery is to you!

In short, I beseech you, I implore you, I am begging: Do
not buzz me for 1B, 2B, 3A, 3B, 4A, 4B, 5A, and 5B. I am
done being a container!

Thank you ever so much for your kind understanding,
empathy, and delivery sensitivity, not to mention your faithful delivery of all parcels for 1A/2A—which I do hope this
request will not in any way inhibit—have a nice day, and
for goodness sake, have the decency to stop peeking in my
window! I know you do it because I can see your shadow
through my drape.

Cordially . . .

Lily laughs and wonders if her note—her entire writing output—is
publishable. Perhaps she could enhance it by adding all the other incur-
sions—sex squeals and barks, the farts and grunts—apartment dwell-
ers' etiquette precludes mentioning. Perhaps it could be published in the
New Yorker's Shouts & Murmurs, which she occasionally reads when one
of her neighbors puts the magazine in recycle. She wonders how much
they pay. Most of the columns sound like they come from a fraternity of
self-conscious smartasses—another kind of herd; they are always by the
same people or occasional movie stars, and they never make her laugh.
She sticks the note in her diary and takes a shower.

Lily lives in a nice Upper West Side neighborhood, but last week, there
were several muggings two blocks west on Broadway. Several dog people
in the park have been talking about signing up for a self-defense class
and one of them asked Lily if she would like to join. There is a teacher
who has offered a private class if they can get a group together. Because
she is spooked that somebody is attacking women walking alone, Lily

says sure, she'll take the class.

Lily has always liked the walk up Broadway. The Saturday morning of her class, she strolls west on Seventy-fourth Street, past Anthony the "Authentic Italian Tailor" whom she never confronted after he kept her waiting a month and finally produced her coat relined with unpressed shiny fabric that puckered at the sides, past the greenery-filled, double-height, casement windows of a brownstone Mrs. Schultz would have lived in. Even though her next turn will be north, Lily sticks to the south side of Seventy-fourth to avoid the mob waiting outside Levain bakery. They are a typical Upper West Side herd of well-educated, articulate, thinking people whose ardor for "world-famous, six-ounce chocolate chip walnut cookies" has been stirred into a craving frenzy by the sugary bakery scent pumped out into the street. High on the smell, they laugh, chatter, and obliviously expand across the entire walkway, blocking patrons of the next-door Laundromat or Max Wax, the second-floor salon that is either run by somebody named Max or, in the current trend of catchy abbreviations, offers the maximum hair removal that a body might require. As Lily passes, she breathes through her mouth, attempting to study the crowd as individuals, to mitigate her judgments and not be so annoyed.

They are all ages—young parents in fashionable sweat suits with squirmy kids precariously balanced on their shoulders; older people in well-worn clothes they've owned for decades who probably bring bags of the sweets to their grandkids.

If she hadn't had the miscarriage—

Banish the thought!

She recently finished reading psychiatrist and Holocaust survivor Viktor Frankl's *Man's Search for Meaning* about how, even in the worst circumstances, if you know your purpose, you can be okay. All these people with offspring know their purpose—to take care of their children. Several of them, sans kids, have that artsy MoMA look—severe blackness highlighted by bright patches of modern art on scarves or heavy artisanal bracelets and multiple jeweled necklaces. Their purpose is probably their art—whether or not anyone else cares about it. If she had stayed at MoMA— but what would she have done? Been a career clerk?

She has no interest in filing and typing.

A dispute has broken out toward the front of the bakery line. Without intending to, Lily has paused in front of a half-demolished apartment building she once visited because her phone number was inexplicably crossed with that of a prostitute who lived there; she wonders where the woman lives now. Lily remembers all the men who phoned her, their soft, expectant voices, their surprise, their disappointment at her coldness as she informed them that yes, they had the right number, but it was reaching the wrong party. She is a cold person. That's just how it is.

From underneath the permanent sidewalk scaffolding on the south side of the street, she mouth-breathes soot from the construction site and watches the bakery scene like a movie. Apparently somebody was holding a place for a friend, but a man with an intellectual's gray ponytail sticking out behind his tweed beret, dressed in a college professor's jacket with patched elbows, says that place-holding is not allowed. He announces this as if he is lecturing and needs to reach the back row of the hall. He is White and the line-breaker is Black and it seems as if this is about to turn into a racial dispute. Remembering the MoMA debacle, Lily moves on.

At the corner of Broadway and Seventy-fourth, she starts to cross, but thinks better of it. Fairway, the neighborhood grocery "like no other market in the world," is particularly hostile on weekends and there will no doubt be more disputes between people battling for discount fruit in the bins outside the store. Even though the self-defense class studio is on the west side of Broadway, she heads north on the east side, past the three Beacons—liquor store, theater, and hotel—past what's now the best discount shoe warehouse in the world where once there was a second-floor pool hall.

Pool balls. No, too heavy. Ping pong balls is what we are, she thinks. Lightweights pinging and ponging up against each other, bouncing back, ricocheting into walls, flying, tumbling, spinning willy-nilly through life. What is the purpose?

If her baby had lived . . .

Stop. After all, there is no guaranteeing a baby would make her feel purposeful. Perhaps, by now, the kid would hate her. Perhaps she'd be a drug addict or in some way impaired. Lily knows from her own experiences as well as those of all the miserable people who have come to her for psychic counseling that, no matter how they present themselves on Facebook, most people are not happy. Whether they know it or not, most people, including Lily, are merely ping pong balls.

Continuing up Broadway, Lily thinks about Facebook. What a revelation for a person who thinks of herself as an isolated spectator. It turned out that she knew enough people from all the groups she'd abandoned (Central Park and Riverside Park dog people, book clubs, knitting, even a couple from the exercise class who also like Kathy Smith and now work out to her DVDs because it's cheaper) to have eighty-two friends. Mostly she is a spectator—"lurking" is what it's called—but recently Lily posted a photo of Wilma with the comment that she's slowed down, and fifty-two people liked or commented!

At Eighty-first Street, her old neighborhood with Philip, she pauses in front of the used book bin of one of the best used bookstores in the world. She has recently become a Percival Everett fan with his book *I Am Not Sidney Poitier*. In it, he did the neat trick of writing himself as a character who has written a real Percival Everett book called *Erasure*. The New York Public Library annoyingly keeps most small press books out of circulation in the research library, so Lily bought a new copy of *Sidney Poitier*—Barnes and Noble, *not* that annoying Amazon—in order to make sure Mr. Everett got compensation for his effort, but now that she has no income, it seems prudent to also buy used when she can find them, and she is searching the bins for *Erasure*.

Nothing. Perhaps after class, she'll walk up to the Barnes & Noble on Eighty-second and see if they have it.

On the other side of Broadway, there is a ruckus outside Zabar's, home of the "most authentic tastes of New York City," in front of what looks like either a voter registry or a fund-raising stand for one of the popular Upper West Side-supported liberal causes—Greenpeace, ACLU, maybe an eco-friendly telephone company. The self-defense class is in a studio on West Eightieth. Lily is half an hour early, so she can wait until the dispute evaporates, leaving no trace of left-wing righteous fisticuffs, or she can circumvent the whole thing by backtracking one block, crossing the street to the wrong side of Eightieth, crossing Broadway and staying on the wrong side of the street until she can jaywalk from the New York Sports Clubs right into the building. She opts for the latter.

Lily has spotted me. I know because I can literally feel her eye energy drilling the back of my head as I hurry west on the north side of Eightieth Street and make a sharp right downstairs to the basement of All Angels' Episcopal Church where my women's self-defense class will be held. I recognize her from her walk—a long-legged, duck-toed, slightly off-kilter, slow-motion lope, but assume/hope she is on her way to the sports club and will not remember me, because I'm not memorable. I'm not being modest or self-effacing. I am merely stating fact. Here is what I look like: a million other New York Jews. Ashkenazi, to be precise, which has nothing to do with religion. Olive skin, long bent nose, frizzy hair, nondescript everything else. The Upper West Side is packed with us. So I'm surprised when I hear the shout.

"Betsy?" yells Lily from across the street.

Damn. Fine. I'll wait. I don't mind being unmemorable. Less obligation. I stop on the second stair and try to make my face affable.

"Hi," she pants, trotting across West Eightieth. "Lily Hogue; remember me? Our Spectators' Club? MoMA? You're Betsy Robinson, right?"

"Of course," I bubble. "I recognized your walk."

I've had a rotten morning. No sleep. My dog was up all night with diarrhea, and I'm way behind on my editing work—a horrible thing by a first-time writer with a boring memoir, but I take anything I can get since losing my magazine job in the not-so-great Recession.

"How have you been?" I ask cordially. "I thought you lived on the East Side."

"Years ago," says Lily, looking really glad to see me. "Are you taking the class? Do you have a dog? I've never seen you in the park. I thought this was all dog people."

The premise of our women's self-defense course is simple, says the teacher, another Ashkenazi with a very tight mouth. (I told you: we're everywhere.) "Women are built differently from men, so to fight off an assailant, we must learn to use those parts of our bodies that are most powerful—hips and thighs. Yup, who'da guessed it? That's our power. And we need to learn verbal skills to avoid ever having to fight. 'Stop!'" she bellows, shoving her hand out with such force that we students flatten against the walls. "Effective, huh?" she says, self-satisfied.

We learn about muscle memory: "You can learn to ride a bike when you're eight, and, even if you don't ride again until you're thirty-five, your body remembers how to do it."

In the first exercises a male co-teacher in a fully padded suit and helmet attacks us from behind in slow motion and we let him take us down, then we kick the hell out of his groin.

We learn to dive to the ground when necessary to best use our hips and thighs as deadly weapons. Lily's dives are surprisingly agile and accurate—her childhood muscle memory apparently well intact.

As the class speeds up, we find ourselves screaming mindlessly in support of each other. Time stops. And after three hours of eye strikes, chin knocks, and groin pulverization, Lily and all of us feel imminently powerful, visible, and sopping wet, so she completely forgets about going to Barnes & Noble for a book called *Erasure*.

"Well, that was informative," she says to me as we limp out. "And imagine, screaming that way in a church."

It's not that I don't like Lily. It's just that I've had no sleep and now my whole body hurts. "Fun," I answer. Also, I'm working on a project—writing a novel, actually—that involves one of the members of our Spectators' Group, and I don't like being in such proximity to someone who knows the truth behind my fiction.

"Listen," says Lily, "I can see you're in a hurry, but I wonder—I heard you are an editor and . . ."

And that's how I end up giving her my card and saying, "Of course, call me whenever you're ready. Or better, email your writing, and I'll take a look and give you an estimate for an edit or consultation." I've learned to mention money up front, especially with clients I know from real life.

That night, a car bomb is discovered near Times Square. Lily—who earlier took a hot shower, then a bath, followed by shadow-fighting with imaginary eye and groin strikes and was so charged up she then masturbated to channel the juice—is watching TV when Mayor Mike Bloomberg makes the bomb announcement at two fifteen Sunday morning.

"A car bomb!" she gasps, petting Wilma who has buried her head under the covers. "Boy, if I had been there, I would have given him a beating." And she imagines bellowing, "9-1-1!" like we did in class, fearlessly alerting not only law enforcement but all the passersby so that they clear out. What a story; she laughs. Story, she thinks. I really should write something. Not a silly superhero fantasy, but something . . . And again, she feels the energy swirling aimlessly. If she channels this into a story, maybe she'll learn her purpose.

CHAPTER 20

Lily has never liked Time Square. The towering buildings with the blaring, blinking neon signs, the shoulder-to-shoulder tourists, the human and concession-stand fried food and bitter coffee stink, so she decides to move the car bomb to the Upper West Side. After all, it's fiction, so she can do as she pleases.

It's May in New York City. Eighty degrees. Low humidity. Easy breathing weather. The view up Broadway is crisp. A flock of gray pigeons soars in counterclockwise circles. There's Verdi Square and the Seventy-second Street IRT subway station. The traffic light at the fork where Broadway splits into upper Broadway and Amsterdam is yellow when the white van crashes into the subway's guardrail. *Ka-boom.* It must have a car bomb in it. Some people freeze; others dive. Bodies fly; bones crack. A horrible accident! A man in a hardhat working on a scaffold above the Tasty Café on Seventy-first vaults to the street and runs to help. Women scream. Babies shriek. What a crazy driver! Call 9-1-1! bellows the hardhat. People on cell phones turn them to record as bodies are dragged out from under the van.

A huge, middle-aged Black woman in violet scrubs hurtles a fragile White woman in a wheelchair across the street away from the accident and parks her next to the benches on Verdi Square. "I've heard these benches have bedbugs," says the White woman, haughtily. "Wait for me," answers the Black woman, and then she waddles as fast as she can back across the street, and that's when there's a second explosion. *Ka-boom.* Bodies fly.

Liza Homer, the woman in the wheelchair, tracks the upsurge and scattering of pigeons as the van bursts into flame. She has always been a watcher, but she forgot her eyeglasses in the restaurant so she can barely see. If she tries very hard, if she breathes low and presses on her uterus, she can feel a little arousal and remember that she was once a member of the scurry, even studying self-defense and once beating up a would-be mugger. But no more. Liza is sixty-five with no juice and no purpose.

Her attendant is clearly dead. Liza knows this from the sound and the heat that is radiating from the other side of the street. She supposes that getting back to the restaurant to retrieve her eyeglasses is no longer an option. She wonders if Medicare will pay for a second eye exam in one year. There must be a record of the prescription somewhere, but for the life of her, she can't remember where, and Nancy, her attendant, took care of those things.

People are rushing across Amsterdam Avenue to the island of Verdi Square to gawk. As the south end of the square fills, Liza edges her chair toward the north end, too far from the action to feel the heat, but close enough to feel the air burst when the third *ka-boom* comes, and that's when she is overwhelmed by déjà vu and painfully aware that this is no accident, and from a vision she once had when she was a professional psychic, she remembers all that is to follow—explosions everywhere, a breakdown of society as we know it, our very democracy in peril.

Having no sense of community, as well as no purpose, Liza has never been politically active. As written earlier, she is a watcher. A spectator. Right now, through rheumy eyes, she watches a group of no doubt politically active teenagers with left-wing Upper West Side parents who have taught them from day one to contribute to society. They are screaming and laughing hysterically, not because they are amused, but because they must release their explosive adolescent juice, their response to the tragedy. There are two fifteen-year-olds, and Liza feels a familiarity as she watches them: One is sparkly-eyed and sure of herself as she points, directing her friend to take a photo of her and to make sure she gets a good angle, so it's clear that sparkle-eyes is part of what will no doubt be a historic act of terrorism on the six o'clock news. Maybe they can even get their video on TV. The girl with the cell phone camera wears a pale yellow parka with a fur-fringed hood—odd because it is completely out of season on such a hot day; is she hiding something? "Cathy, now!" yells sparkle-eyes. "What's the matter with you?" Sparkle-eyes has perfectly symmetrical features, a sharp little nose, and short brown hair curled back to expose gold hoop earrings. "Cathy!"

But Cathy is frozen. A spectator. She has been hiding how useless she is.

So, too, is Liza useless. Despite pressing on her uterus so hard that it leaves a bruise, she dies and will not be found until the six o'clock news crews come for an on-site report and try to shoo her away.

The End

After several years of freelance editing, I have learned that people write for various reasons, but they don't always know what they are. Some people believe if they tell their story, other people will hear them and love them. Others feel a kind of tension about all that they've been through and they imagine if they can channel it into a story, it will help people. There are always those that want fame and money; these are usually people with no experience whatsoever in publishing, and many times they don't even read. There are people who feel compelled to write and never actually do; instead they join writers' communities and talk about how blocked they are and imagine if they can become part of a good writing group—an oxymoron, since you could not find a more requisitely solitary form of expression—they will be able to write something that the world is waiting to hear. And then there are people who just want to get the thing out—to have a release. So not all writing is for publication. My job as an experienced editor is not only to edit but sometimes to know more than the writer does about why they're writing, or, if not, to help them find out by asking questions, being diplomatic, kind, and nonjudgmentally encouraging.

"This is absolutely awful," I tell Lily. "No plot, no character development; setups with no resolutions, no story." We are sitting in her parlor, which isn't at all what I expected. So warm. So much beautiful old stuff, not that I know anything about art or antiques. I feel comfortable enough to be honest: "In short, your writing irredeemably sucks."

Lily laughs so hard she has to pee. "I thought so," she says, excusing herself and running for the bathroom with her hand between her legs.

And it is at that moment that I know we are going to be good friends.

"Look, no way am I going to charge you for this," I tell her when she returns. "It's not editable. Why don't we just go on dog walks, and we can talk?" I remember her psychic gifts from our group and I wouldn't mind hearing her take on things. Win/win.

"So let me get this straight," I say on our first dog walk, "you don't want anything?"

"That's right," Lily answers.

It's a month since we met at the self-defense class and then had our consultation—it takes that long for loners to reach out to one another—and we are meandering with our dogs, Wilma and Maya, down Central Park's Literary Walk.

"So what's the point?" I ask. "I mean, why get out of bed?"

Lily gestures with her chin toward Wilma, who apparently is walking much better after a month of rest following diagnosis of a slipped disc.

"Yeah, well there's the dogs. But you really don't want anything?"

It's June 2010, and, according to the government, 431,000 jobs were added last month, but I still don't have one and have given up any hope of getting one. I've accepted that freelance is my new normal.

"If you don't mind my asking, and as I said, I'm not looking to be your editor, why did you even think you wanted to write? Or did you—if you don't want anything?"

And Lily tells me about ghost Harmony.

As I said in our Spectators' Club meeting a billion time slices ago, I accept all levels of life in the different slices of so-called time (and I didn't get that from reading quantum mechanics to cure my insomnia). And I accept that there can be crossovers.

We walk silently for a minute and then stop in front of the Robert Burns statue. "He makes writing look so romantic," I say, releasing Maya so she can nose around the base for a place to pee. "I'm sure Harmony didn't know what a terrible writer you are."

"I think Harmony looks like a half-Black Hillary Clinton," says Lily, unleashing Wilma. "Did you ever notice that?"

"Maybe so," I answer. "I voted for her in the primary. Hillary, not Harmony. Not Obama."

"Got it," says Lily. "Me, too."

And we both laugh.

"But I'm okay with Obama," I say.

"Things work out the way they're supposed to, I guess," answers Lily, shrugging. And we walk on.

"I like that Walter Scott has a dog," I say, as we pass his statue. "Although they really don't like it when you ignore them in order to write."

Lily stops in front of Scott's identifying plaque and pretends to read the lengthy history. Then we head north along the mall toward the Bandshell, breathing in the perfume of the Olmstead flowerbed and the canopy of Elm leaves that shade the path on either side. June is brutal in New York City, but the Elms always offer a respite.

"Are you on Facebook?" Lily asks.

"I lurk," I answer.

"Me, too."

"Who is Fitz-Greene Halleck?" I ask as Maya and Wilma stop in front of his statue. Like all the other writers, he looks loftily into the ether, waiting for inspiration with no apparent concern about hunger or paying rent.

"No idea," says Lily. "Probably some poet. I don't read poetry."

"Me neither. Do you want to be Facebook friends?"

"Okay," says Lily.

And that ends our first sojourn.

There is nothing like lurking on Facebook to realize how outside the culture you've been all your life—all the pop singers you've never heard of now mourned by millions after their deaths by overdose, all the movies and sit-coms you never watched that form the fabric of most people's lives. Lily and I share this. The unspoken knowing brings us closer, despite the fact that we don't see each other for several months and merely comment on each other's rare and culturally oblivious posts.

It is fall when we meet for our second walk in front of the statue of Hans Christian Andersen with his duck on the west side of the Little Boat Pond in Central Park. After the sparest of hellos, no hugs or any kind of physical greeting—another preference Lily and I share—we circle clockwise with our dogs, north to east, but stop like synchronized walkers and turn to look back at a familiar person, whose small mutt is sitting atop the mushroom of the bronze Alice in Wonderland statue, based on the drawings of John Tenniel with no attribution. "Leslie Kove," we murmur in one voice. And without glancing at each other, we backtrack to say hello.

It's been a long time.

Like three human cells with three canine satellites, we coagulate into one being and change our route, strolling north behind Alice, past the Soccer for Tots class for Upper East Side yuppie offspring, through the tunnel and toward Dog Hill, a popular off-leash playing field that the Central Park Conservancy insists on calling Cedar Hill and trolling with Park Patrol Nazis.

Because I'm feeling affable and like a psychopath if I don't confess it, I tell Leslie that I wrote her into my first novel, *Plan Z by Leslie Kove*, about a girl with PTSD, and she blushes, but doesn't kill me.

"Funny," she says. "I thought I was my own creator."

Then I admit to both Leslie and Lily that I wrote Harmony Rogers—even her death in 9/11—in another novel, *Cats on a Pole*.

"Sounds sexy," says Leslie. "If you're into felines dancing."

I decide not to push my luck and keep to myself the fact that I'm currently working on a book starring Zelda McFigg. And then Lily tells Leslie and me about Lucresse's death in 1990 of leukemia, and, although I feel as if it's my turn to speak again, I don't mention that my late mother who died of leukemia wrote a book starring a protagonist named Lucresse that I one day intend to edit and publish. So many coincidences stretch credulity.

There is an empty pause.

"So what are you doing for a living these days?" I ask Leslie, as I'm always curious about other people who manage to be in the park midday.

"I type," she answers. "Nights in a law office—for the last ten years. Pays well. I hate it."

Lily picks up the pace, making a sharp left up Dog Hill and we follow. "This will probably sound silly," Lily says to Leslie, "but years ago I had a dream about— Well, not really about. Well, the thing is, I think your brother gave me a message for you."

"Peter?" gasps Leslie, tearing up. "I almost never even think about him anymore. What an asshole for going to Vietnam and— "

"He said to tell you he gave up, but you shouldn't," Lily interrupts. "He said there was no point in Vietnam, but you shouldn't give up."

Nobody says anything. Leslie swallows hard. And we walk on.

At the top of Dog Hill is a clot of towering fir trees that marks a stopping place, a pinetum of calm amidst the aromatic but dead needles and cones. We linger, watching the dogs—Wilma, Maya, and now Leslie's Spud—ignoring each other as they nose and mark. Like us, they seem to know each other without need of small talk.

"Is that Paul Simon?" asks Leslie, spotting a small man with wispy gray hair sticking out the sides of a baseball cap, determinedly jogging north along the park's East Drive.

"He lives in the neighborhood," say Lily and I simultaneously.

"Once I saw him in the old A&P on Broadway," I say.

"Before it turned into the Food Emporium, and then an empty building because nobody would pay the inflated rent?" says Leslie to prove how long she's lived on the Upper West Side.

Ignoring her, I continue, "An old lady was screaming and waving her cane at him. I think he'd bumped her or something and he looked so surprised, like he couldn't believe she didn't recognize him. And he was loving it. She was so angry she almost hit him, but he ducked."

"What's it all for?" asks Leslie after a beat.

"Being famous?" I ask.

"No. Everything. Like writing 'The Sound of Silence' or 'Kodachrome' or 'American Tune' when people just get mad at you in supermarkets and none of it matters?"

"Who knew you were a Simon fan?" I answer, surprised. "I thought we were all culturally oblivious."

"I think I know what you mean," says Lily, ignoring me. "Like why have psychic prophecies if you can't do anything about them?"

"When people learn my last name, they always sing, 'Here's to you, Mrs. Robinson' like it doesn't matter that I'm not a Mrs. and have heard that a billion times before," I say, watching Paul Simon disappear around the north bend in the road. "I could be world famous, but all they hear is the Robinson and their joke."

"What are we doing here?" asks Lily.

And nobody answers.

Over the course of many similar walks and mosaic conversations, Leslie, Lily, and I marry each other. We become what others might term a *folie à trois*, witnessing each other and all that we observe with no idea why we're watching. With no premeditation, we become a true Spectators' Club.

CHAPTER 21

Obama and Biden win a second term and we Spectators approve. The CIA director resigns after the scandal of an extra-marital affair with a reporter and Leslie goes on and on about the insanity of that being more unforgiveable than the possible inappropriate sharing of classified information. North Korea successfully launches a rocket; next step is an intercontinental ballistic missile to the USA and we don't care because they seem so far away and we're more interested in finding our mysterious *raison d'être*. A twenty-year-old gunman kills twenty-six people, including twenty little children, at a Connecticut elementary school, but the good news is that the US economy shows consistent growth after the Recession with the lowest unemployment rate in four years so perhaps Lily, Leslie, and I will be okay after all. Same sex marriage is approved by the Supreme Court and we joke about a threesome. The Black Lives Matter movement explodes after a rash of police killings of unarmed Black men, and Lily begins attending concerts—anything Bach—all over the city. Occasionally she invites me to come as her guest. Leslie is too busy for entertainment since she's become involved with a program to help inner-city kids learn to present themselves well to White corporate America, thereby procuring a future with good jobs and not getting killed. When she invites Lily and me to go with her to an event where kids and cops learn to hear each other, we say, sure, why not.

The famous Apollo Theater is a sea of plush red carpet and upholstery with gold walls and balustrades, and we are in red heaven at the top of the top balcony near the ceiling, surrounded by more laughing, chatting, joking navy-blue-dress-uniformed police officers than I knew existed— many of them recent Academy graduates who have come to this event, Operation Conversation: Cops & Kids, because it is compulsory. The atmosphere is festive, and it takes the emcee, a Black psychologist who founded this program, a little while to get everybody quiet and explain what is going to happen.

What happens is just what the title says: White cops and Black and Hispanic kids sit on folding chairs and one by one start to share with each other how they feel about their mutual confrontations. Leslie, perched on the edge of her plush red seat, is riveted, attentive. I listen like a reporter, because, who knows, one day I may want to fictionalize this. And Lily has an odd, frozen, wide-eyed owl look. Even behind her thick glasses, I can tell that she is crying.

"What?" I whisper, nudging her with my elbow, but she shakes her head and blinks me off.

It turns out two of the cops are related—uncle and nephew—and as they speak, Lily starts to tremble, so I lean in again.

"Sh!" she snaps.

"Okay," I say. "Okay."

The older cop, a detective named Ernie, talks about how he felt after his brother, the nephew's father, was shot and killed on a domestic violence call, and how proud he is of Ed Junior, but sometimes he feels an overwhelming responsibility to his late brother and he wishes he'd talked Ed Junior out of joining the force, as well as his own son who has just graduated from the Academy and is in the audience. A male *huzzah* erupts in the back of the orchestra seats underneath our balconies, and before Ed Junior can answer, one of the kids says that's fine for a cop, but what about the family of the people who get shot when the police break into the wrong apartment and mistake someone like *his* uncle who was just reaching for his wallet to get his identification? The kid starts to get out of his chair, but the psychologist emcee breaks in to compliment everybody on their raw and honest sharing which is what we all need in order to understand each other's pain.

"I *know* them," whispers Lily.

"Who?"

"Both of them. Ernie Shoren and his dead brother Ed. They lived in my rooming house. Remember when they came in when we were having the Spectators meeting?" And awash in the mysterious sadness of decades ago, she rocks in pain.

I only vaguely recollect but I nod. "Absolutely. Right. They came in the room."

"I guess they became cops," she says, and then laughs at the obviousness and blows her nose. "And Ed's dead and has an adult child! I'm just shocked, that's all."

"Sh," hiss some civilians in the row in front of us, but a couple of the young navy-blue-suited Academy graduates smile and give us a thumbs-up to let us know we haven't offended anybody and that they are affable cops.

After the program is over, we and hundreds of New York's newest Finest spill onto West 125th Street between Adam Clayton Powell Jr. Boulevard and Frederick Douglass Boulevard in the heart of Harlem.

"Do you want to wait and talk to them?" I ask Lily.

She shakes her head and, looking straight ahead, the three of us plow through the cops and kids, and once clear of the crowd, silently hike to the subway.

"It's just that I feel so old," Lily says a few blocks later. "They have adult children. It's a shock."

"Do you want to volunteer with the All Stars?" asks Leslie helpfully.

"The what?" we ask.

Leslie laughs. "I told you about a million times. The organization that's behind this whole thing."

"Right," says Lily.

"Not really," I say. Not because I don't think it's a good cause, but I'm afraid to commit time to any work that doesn't pay.

"Maybe if you started helping people, you'd feel more purpose," Leslie almost snaps. And we both realize she has changed.

It happened so gradually, we hadn't noticed. She spends weekends in workshops with inner-city kids. And last month, she started going tango dancing. She's asked Lily and me to join her, but we've shrugged it off. And ever since the debut of Sarah Palin, she's been reading the *New York Times* and talking about current events.

Rather than inspire us, it's made us feel guilty. Because we—Lily and I—would rather feel like purposeless spectators than do anything about it.

CHAPTER 22

When Lily gets home from the outing at the Apollo Theater, she walks Wilma, mouth breathing to avoid the pungent rubbery asphalt smell from where they recently repaved the street in front of her building. Ever since the experience with ghost Harmony, her sense of smell has gone nuts.

Even though she still hates her dead-end job, Leslie seems to be fired up these days, not only with the inner-city kids, but with her tango dancing and other projects; maybe the message from her brother had an impact. Betsy is an amusing curmudgeon. She has her freelance work, although she never talks about it and gives the impression that destitution is a moment away. Betsy has an edge—dangerous for no obvious reasons; just an aura. But she's certainly not juiceless. And she seems sincerely interested in life, as opposed to the alternative.

After they return from their pee walk, Lily unleashes Wilma and closes the front window but still can feel the asphalt burn in her nostrils. She pours a bowl of kibble and sets it on the floor, turns on *The Paul Simon Anthology* double CD set, clicks "repeat whole CD sequence," and eats a bowl of uncooked oatmeal with barely ripe blackberries and almond milk which most people would find boring but to her is like dessert. She loves the contrast on her tongue of the grain with the creamy, nutty liquid and the bitter squirt of the berries, but as Paul Simon regales her with sounds of silence and words about how we're all slipping and sliding away and only God knows what's going on, she finds herself gripping her glass bowl so hard it breaks.

After the initial shock, she cleans up the shards, undresses, and masturbates as Simon sings how we're all shattered and trying to get some rest but still everything will be all right because we'll all be welcomed at Graceland. And even though Lily never reads poetry, as she orgasms she realizes that Paul Simon wrote everything there is to know in one song, yet he still jogs like a person lugging rocks and is attacked by old ladies in supermarkets. Then she falls asleep to Simon and a boy named Julio down by the schoolyard.

As the music fades, she is clinging by her fingernails to a sheer perpendicular wall of rock, miles above a forest canopy, her body twisted like a pretzel, her legs flailing in empty air.

"Bella!" shouts a familiar man's voice that she can't place. And even though her name is not Bella, she cranes her neck out of its pretzel curve to see a man hurtling down from the clouds, his face stretched out to kiss her.

"Bernie?" she asks. "Why did you rob me?"

And shrugging, Bernie Madoff drops, disappearing like a wrecking ball loosed from its cable into the canopy of trees below.

Then a man she's never seen before but who she knows is Madoff's dead-by-suicide son materializes. She marvels that the resemblance is in the eyes only and suddenly notices that she is wearing an old-fashioned black dress with a frilly lace collar. "He couldn't help it," pleads Mark Madoff, dressed in old-fashioned green blouse and black tights and floating next to her but slightly above, his neck craned backward, twisted in an impossible position as if to catch her in a kiss. As they float back to back, impossible lovers, he begs, "Help my brother Andy. Can you help him? Please. He doesn't deserve this. He's like Peter. Just tell him to—"

And Lily jerks herself awake to the serenade of Paul Simon, who has circled back to "The Sound of Silence."

"Fuck."

The light-up alarm clock shows it's three a.m. "I have to pee," she mumbles to Wilma who is looking perplexed. "Sorry. Go back to sleep."

Shocked by the movement of her own reflection in the closet mirror and bumping into the dresser, stubbing her toe on the side chair, she staggers out to the living room, turns off the CD player, pees, writes in her diary, and slips back under the covers.

In the morning, she goes downstairs to her parlor, opens the window, sits on her upholstered session chair, grounding her feet on the Persian rug, as if she is doing psychic counseling, breathes deeply, inhaling asphalt, closes her eyes, and pronounces to anybody who might be hanging in the ether, "I am done. I do not want to do it anymore. I am out of the psychic business. No more messages from dead people to living people. Leave me alone!" And a ping pong ball falls out of nowhere, bouncing off the top of Chagall's "The Birthday" print frame and rolling under the sofa.

"Fuck," she says and takes Wilma for a walk.

CHAPTER 23

In September 2014, Andrew Madoff, Bernie's second son, dies of cancer. Although some of Madoff's victims have recouped some of their stolen money, Lily has not. She wants nothing to do with the Madoffs, is satisfied with her checking account and the floorboard money, and would prefer to forget the whole debacle.

According to the Labor Department, the U.S. economy added 144,000 jobs in the first month of 2014—an increase from the 74,000 jobs added in December 2013, but lower than many economists predicted. The unemployment rate has continued to fall and is the lowest since the Great Recession began in November 2008. However, this is due to so many people dropping out of the work force—like Lily.

Determined to follow Leslie's example to get out more, Lily decides to attend an Eighty-second Street Barnes & Noble talk about a new book about Marc Chagall. She still hasn't bought Percival Everett's *Erasure*, so she can kill two book tasks with one visit. Strange as it sounds, Lily is still grateful to Bernie Madoff for the "Birthday" print and feels a little guilty for ignoring Mark's message for his brother. When he said Andrew was like Peter, although she would like to deny it, she knew exactly what he was communicating: like Leslie's brother Peter, Andrew had stopped trying. Even so, what could she have done? Gone to Andrew's hospital room with a message from his dead brother? She'd have been thrown out and locked up, which she recently heard from Leslie, who heard from Betsy, whom she hasn't heard from since the night they went to the Apollo, was the fate of Zelda McFigg—a looney bin in Vermont. "How does Betsy know?" Lily asked Leslie.

"She said she wrote it," answered Leslie, rolling her eyes.

The Chagall book talk is apparently not popular so Lily has her choice of metal folding chairs. If she sits in the front row in front of the podium, she will feel observed by the writer, and what if she doesn't enjoy the talk? With so many empty chairs near the front, if she sits too far back, it will look like she is uninterested and she may offend him. The middle chairs are occupied, and if she sits right next to somebody, well, that's intrusive. Finally she decides to sit in the middle row, on the aisle with one empty chair between her and another person—even if it means an obstructed view of the author because the man right in front of her has a top bun.

"Is this seat taken?" asks a familiar voice.

"No," answers Lily, who has been caught cleaning her glasses and is temporarily blind. But she doesn't really care to make eye contact because sitting in an empty chair right next to her when there are so many empties is tacky.

"Lily?" asks the voice, rising theatrically on the second syllable.

Bobbling her glasses, she manages to get them on over one eye—enough to see an older man with tousled, graying, yellow hair whose once crooked teeth are now gleaming perfection. She looks at him quizzically.

"Philip," says Philip, grabbing her shoulder, and it is all Lily can do to quash her muscle memory-driven impulse to smash his chin and strike his eyes.

"Philip?" she says, drawing back and crossing her legs. "How nice to see you. What are you doing here? I didn't know you liked art."

"In the neighborhood," says Philip, shrugging, flashing teeth, and crossing one unironed khaki-panted leg over the other as he glances down at his phone.

"You're in the neighborhood?"

"Yeah. I never moved. Rent stabilized. I'm no idiot. So how are you? You look a lot older, but if I stare, I can still see the girl. You really should pencil in your eyebrows though."

"Good to see you too," says Lily dryly.

"Ha, I like that. You're cheeky in your old age." Philip alternately peruses his smartphone and the rest of the room but continues chatting. "I work in advertising now, but you probably know that."

How would I know, thinks Lily. Is he famous?

"Remember that pool hall on Seventy-ninth? I was hanging out there, making jokes. A lot of the comics did. And someone heard me and said

I'd be good at copywriting—that's writing ads and stuff. I ended up being the go-to guy for table sports: pool, pinball, ping pong. 'Block it, chop it, do anything but drop it. Paddle Palace for all your ping pong needs.' I wrote that."

"Very catchy," says Lily, and that's when the Barnes & Noble emcee steps up and blows into the microphone.

The talk is interesting. Despite Philip's constant movement as he scans the audience and scrolls his phone, she keeps her eyes glued to the author and even takes notes, just to enhance her concentration, although she has no intention of buying the book.

She learns that Marc and Bella Chagall were madly in love and much of his work, like her beloved "The Birthday" print, is a celebration of romantic love. In fact, years after Chagall painted it, his wife described it in her own memoir, *First Encounter*:

> "Spurts of red, blue, white, black. Suddenly you tear me
> from the earth, you yourself take off from one foot. You
> rise, you stretch your limbs, you float up to the ceiling. Your
> head turns about and you make mine turn. You brush my
> ear and murmur."

Lily would love to give in to the swoon in her chest, but Philip nudges her and points to a woman at the end of their row.

"I used to date her. Complete bitch."

Lily ignores him.

After the talk is over, Philip pauses mid-rise from his chair, flashes a blinding smile, and snaps a one-handed selfie of himself and the literary audience. "Facebook and Instagram. To show I'm cultchah-ed," he quips. Then he attaches himself to Lily as she starts to stand. "Come with me for coffee," he orders. "We've got business to discuss." And Lily goes blank.

Business? Is this still about money? For goodness sake, their sham marriage was over four decades ago, and that's when she notices Martin Bratmore staring at her from a book cover, face-out on the shelf right in front of her.

"Are you coming?" asks Philip, impatient. And then following her focus. "What? You interested in jazz? That guy was a legend. Get it. I can wait."

Feeling as if she's made of helium, Bella in "The Birthday," she floats toward the shelf, and she could swear she's bobbing, hovering high above everything as she pulls the book out and reads the jacket copy:

> Legendary trumpet jazzman Martin Bratmore, 1951–2012, set the jazz world on fire with his covers of Miles Davis's "Kind of Blue" album, but he may best be remembered for his contribution to research for ALS, known commonly as Lou Gehrig's Disease, the progressive debilitating neurological disorder that killed him and infects his two adult sons, who have written this stirring biography (with remixed CDs of Bratmore's best-known performances) memorializing his unflagging commitment to music and medicine—the proceeds of which will go to the Martin Bratmore Foundation to Cure ALS.

Pop goes the helium balloon called Lily Hogue. She returns the book to the shelf, and what follows feels like a dream.

"Come on," says Philip. "I'm paying." And without waiting, he hooks an arm through hers and steers her in and out of the literature aisles toward the escalator in the middle of the third floor.

"Wait," says Lily, suddenly coming to in front of the *W* books.

"Look, it's eight o'clock. I gotta go to work in the morning."

On impulse, Lily pretends to be interested in a book she's never seen before. A paperback with a painting of a pince-nez bespectacled, pensive man in a black overcoat. *Stoner* is the title. John Williams is the author. She's never heard of him or the book.

Philip raises his eye brows. "Jazz, drugs, rock 'n' roll? Maybe we should've stayed together."

Ignoring this and using both hands to hold the book and her purse so that there is no space for Philip to grab her, she marches ahead of him toward the escalator.

"I've got to pay for this," she says when they reach the first floor. Why can't she just tell him to leave her alone? Something unpleasant is coming; she can feel it. Weaving through book displays to the cashier, she moves slowly, buying time, and Philip stays right with her.

"*Stoner!*" says the boy at the register. He looks like a very young graduate student, the kind of boy Lily should have appealed to when she was young, but she never thought to think that somebody like that would be interested in her. "This is one of the greatest books ever written."

Philip snorts and checks the time on his phone.

"Well, then I can't wait to read it," says Lily, demurely offering her credit card.

"Enjoy having your world rocked," says the boy knowingly. He hands her the receipt, and Philip again takes her arm, guiding her toward the exit at the front.

"There's a coffee shop right here," says Lily, eying the stairs to their left. She knows they serve almost no food, so perhaps this can be quick.

"Starbucks," pronounces Philip, and impels her out of the store into the street-light-lit night.

"Who'da thought our neighborhood would get so posh?" says Philip, setting coffee down in front of Lily and sitting opposite her at the window table that looks out at nighttime on their old block, West Eighty-first Street.

"What's this about, Philip?" asks Lily, sipping what she hopes is decaf. "We're both old. The marriage was a mistake. Can't we just let this disappear?" And that's when she remembers she forgot to look for *Erasure*. It's a small press book, so most likely Barnes & Noble doesn't even carry it. Maybe she'll buy it online. She shrugs.

"You just had a whole conversation with yourself that had nothing to do with me," says Philip with something between wonder and resentment. "I used to hate that."

Lily watches the ripples in his jaw as he grinds his porcelain caps. He's still handsome in that hayseed way, but now she can see meanness, bitterness, the firmly held belief that life has stolen his inheritance, and suddenly she realizes this was always there.

"So what were you doing at a talk about Chagall?" she asks to deflect whatever is coming.

Philip gauges her and the teeth grinding gives way to a flinty smile. She can feel him evaluating the lines in her face, her drooping jawline, even her breasts underneath her thick winter jacket. "It's a convenient way to meet women," he quips.

"Cute." Lily sips her coffee.

Bach's Concerto for Two Violins and Orchestra in D minor starts on muzak and Lily suddenly experiences a collision of feelings—bliss and dread. Philip is showing her who he is and always was. The smartphone glances are constant. He has all the tics and herd addictions of their time.

"I don't suppose we're having sex tonight," he says, feeling her out with his eyes over his coffee cup. It's a real question with a jokey delivery.

Lily chokes on her coffee and manages to catch it in her napkin.

"Didn't think so," continues Philip as if this is normal and it has not been more than forty years since she walked out. "After all, legally we're still married."

Again, Lily gags.

"I figured you knew from your goon who sent me the divorce papers. I didn't see the point of signing once my fiancée dumped me. So I guess you did pretty well to be with that Madoff crowd. Sorry about that, by the way. I guess you lost a bundle."

Lily can't breathe. She is gripping her cardboard cup.

"You're going to destroy that," says Philip casually.

Lily wills her fingers to relax and, with her other hand, fingers the new book in her bag.

"I don't even know what you did after you left. How you made all that money," Philip continues.

"Real estate," mumbles Lily's mouth, because it is partially true and may satisfy him. Her mind froze on the divorce papers.

"Funny," says Philip. "I never saw you as a sales-type person."

"I owned some real estate—inherited," coughs Lily, because although her brain is subarctic, it still can't bear an inaccuracy. "I sold it."

"Nice."

"I don't have any money to give you, if that's what you're after," she says, recovering her voice. "So you might as well just sign the papers."

Philip's face is doing an odd crumbling thing. His eyes remain steely, but his nose is pushing down toward his mouth which is twitching in and out of an almost imperceptible frown. "You know, I'm a good guy," he says almost plaintively.

"I know," says Lily, softening—perhaps more due to the fact that the eighth movement, the andante Concerto for Two Violins, has just started.

"You just walked out," he whines.

"You're right," she answers. He looks and sounds like a small child, but she wants to finish this. Once and for all. But the music, the music. The duet, the dipping and dancing and lovemaking, why does this feel so complicated? She does not love this man.

"I know you never loved me."

It's as if he's in her mind. Lily starts to tighten her hand around her cup, then puts both hands in her bag, gripping the new book instead.

"But I was a good guy, a nice guy." He pauses and briefly brightens. "Maybe a small payment for pain and suffering?"

Lily tosses her head back in disgust.

"Just kidding. God! You never did have a sense of humor. But you still have a very nice neck when you arch it that way."

"I need to get home to walk my dog," says Lily dryly.

"You have a dog?" asks Philip, sipping like nothing will stop him from taking all the time he needs. "Nice." Then, as the ninth movement of the concertos, the crazy duet chase, erupts on the muzak, as if overcome by a long-suppressed wave of grief, he grips the sides of the table with both hands, and leaning forward in a way that reminds Lily of when he was seventeen and desperate to see his name on that casting sheet saying that he, Philip from Boston, was going to play the best Tom ever seen in *The Glass Menagerie*, he lets loose: "How could you have treated me so badly? I didn't deserve any of it. The leaving and all the other stuff."

"Other stuff?" asks Lily, unable to stop herself.

"Your aloofness. Yes, I know that word. Don't look so surprised. You never even tried to be with me. And all that B.S. about how you didn't want anything. Bull! You wanted plenty and mostly it was to be left alone, to be above all the messy humans like me because you believe you're superior. You said you weren't competitive. Bull! You were always competing to win the prize for the most aloof, self-sufficient human being on the planet. Hell, you didn't even want sex with me—or probably any other man for that matter. It is men, right? You're not a— "

Numb, Lily shakes her head.

"I'll bet you only get off on yourself; probably would win the prize for best masturbator in the universe, cause that's what you are, Lily. A master-baiter. You bait and master! Ha! Ha-ha-ha! You've never cared to be with anybody but yourself. Just like your mother. Yeah, I noticed. No wonder your father was such an asshole. I heard about them and your brothers from my mother, by the way. Sorry for your loss."

Lily can't move.

Philip heaves a great sigh, lets go of the table, and leans back in his chair. Then like a stop-motion movie, his face melts into an almost goofy smile. "I guess I've been holding onto that a long time, as my shrink would say. They say you've got to express this stuff or it'll wreak holy hell on your system." He claps a big hand over his heart. "I'm into alternative medicine—ever since the heart attack scare. Fuck Western medicine. I see this holistic guy and he turned me on to a lot of New Age wisdom. Boy, it felt good expressing all that. Oh, and on the bright side—" He brushes his hair off his forehead the way he used to do during his act to cover the dead silence when the audience didn't laugh. "Herman, that's my holistic doctor, says always to balance things—yin and yang, etcetera—so you don't create more bad karma. After you left, I got a job. I realized I had no talent for comedy, so I was actually working in that pool hall I told you about. And that led to—well, you know, being the go-to guy for table sports. I grew up. I guess it's the ping-pong ball effect."

Lily wills herself to breathe.

"Herman always talks about that—how all our actions, whether we're aware of them or not, have reactions and sometimes even though they may seem like bad things, they pong somebody else into something good. So you ponged me, Lily. I guess I should say thank you."

"Listen, I really do have to walk my dog," says Lily robotically.

"Sure, sure. Well, listen, it was great seeing you." He stands abruptly and, scrolling his phone, he walks out of Starbucks into the night.

When she gets home, Lily plods up and down the dark block with Wilma. She is numb. A head in a bubble floating somewhere near the top of a body that drags like dead weight. Wilma looks at her, curious, but she has seen this before, so when they return home, the dog noses around the kibble canister to remind Lily to feed her. Remembering that she almost forgot, Lily opens the canister, her hands like baseball mitts as she reaches in with the measuring cup. Her motor skills have abandoned her when she pours the kibble into Wilma's bowl, and half of it bounces onto the floor where Wilma scarfs it up.

Perhaps if she writes in her diary—about everything: the loss of her baby a second time via the news about ALS, the loss of a family who never belonged to her so she'd never mourned them, the loss of a marriage that never should have been, the loss of her fantasy that she never wanted anything so there was no way to miss it. She writes, but the sentences are dead, words without pulse—Betsy was right; she's a terrible writer—and still she is aware that she is not quite here. Although Lily feels no arousal or interest in anything physical, let alone her bloodless body, to turn on her "juice" and thereby switch on the pulse, she drags herself to the bedroom, falls backwards onto the mattress, pulls up her skirt, pushes out of her underwear, and starts to rub—only to remember Philip's words, shutting off the possibility of sensation. Dead. He was right. She is dead in her crotch. Dead in her heart. Dead. Just like her mother. She always has been. It's not, as Philip said, that she feels superior to everybody. It's that she is too dead—not here enough to even know that her removal reads as arrogance, and perhaps that *is* a form of arrogance, although she can't articulate why.

At a loss for what to do, she picks up her new book, *Stoner*, and from the first words about this man, an assistant college professor in the English Department of the University of Missouri named William Stoner—a man who was held "in no particular esteem when he was alive"—she is mesmerized. The book is simply his life and death. He goes to school for agriculture, but meets a teacher, Archer Sloane, who makes Lily think of Mrs. Schultz. Sloane wakes up Stoner to his inborn passion, literature, just as Mrs. S tried so hard to wake up Lily; however the problem there was that the passion for psychic counseling belonged to Mrs. S, not Lily, and try as she did—because she loved Mrs. S and believed her wise—Lily could not maintain life through it. Stoner marries a woman named Edith, whose damage he seems to understand, even see beneath to a better person by the end of the book, but she robs him of all he loves—as does his life. And yet . . . and yet . . .

At first light—Lily has lost track of time—when Stoner dies, she feels as if she has lost the love of her life:

> There was a softness around him, and a languor crept
> upon his limbs. A sense of his own identity came upon him
> with a sudden force, and he felt the power of it. He was
> himself, and he knew what he had been.

Oh, to know that, thinks Lily. To know just that.

But then there is Edith, a woman who cannot love, who is so afraid of love that she must destroy it in anyone around her. A woman who is dead. Like Lily?

Horrified, Lily vaults out of bed, races to the shower, and as she is soaping herself, murmurs out loud—to herself? To the ether? It doesn't matter. "It isn't me. I've never hurt anyone. Not even Philip. I didn't stay long enough. Not the baby either. It was good it slid out of me early. It did the right thing. I'm dead, but I've never taken anyone with me. At least there's that."

CHAPTER 24

By spring of 2015, I wondered if Lily had decided she didn't like us. We—Leslie Kove and I (Betsy)—hadn't seen her in the park for most of the winter of 2014 to 2015. Occasionally I called but usually got her answering machine and didn't leave a message. Neither Lily nor I had the texting or even the smartphone habit, and I figured eventually I'd run into her and ask what was up. Maya, my dog, liked Leslie's dog, Spud, so when Leslie wasn't in a hurry to get to inner-city kids volunteer work or a Bernie Sanders campaign activity, which was rare, we sometimes made plans to walk in the early morning when the dogs could play off leash. Just as many times as we made plans, Leslie broke them. I accept this; after all, I'd written her and therefore had firsthand experience with her difficulty in regard to linear thought and follow-through.

By late April, however, I'll admit it. I was lonely. After Bernie Sanders had formally declared his candidacy for president, Leslie was in an envelope-stuffing frenzy. Add to that that my on- and off-again man friend of more than a decade (another story) finally mentioned that we didn't seem to care for each other and he was moving to Colorado. To be honest, it was a relief. I never wanted to be married or even be part of a pair; once my estrogen subsided and I no longer erupted in bouts of horniness, I realized that I had never even fantasized about sharing my life, space, and every decision with a man. What I wanted was what I had—autonomy and life with a dog. This is the nature of some loners, and I accept it. However, I remembered how nice it had been to have the company of two like-minded women, so when I was cleaning out my closet and found an old Ouija board that my friend Edith had given to me because it spooked her, I thought it might be a good excuse to get us all—Leslie, Lily, and me—together and ask for answers to life's great questions—not that I believed in such things.

"We could bring our dogs," I say to Leslie on the phone.

"All right," says Leslie. "But you call her and see if she really wants to.

I've dreamt about her a bunch of times and have a feeling she's in a dark place, and I'm finally in a really good place and I need all my positivity to fight for democracy."

It turns out Leslie is prescient. Lily is almost incommunicative. Wilma died in her sleep over the winter.

"Oh, Lily, I'm so sorry," I tell her. I feel horrible that I never left messages, but I also know that isolation was Lily's choice all these months, and if she is going to share the reasons why, that too has to be her choice. And she doesn't. In fact, she sounds like death. Polite death. So without intruding on her misery, I mention the Ouija board and how Leslie and I would like to—

And I barely get the words out when she's saying, "Yes, come over. We can do it in my parlor. And bring the dogs!"

Although Leslie and I are now in our sixties, both of us have a kid-like, older woman quality. Neither of us has married or borne children, nor have we followed traditional work trajectories, so we've never had to deal with professional relationships, climbing ladders, or exhausted uteruses and drooping breasts. We've never negotiated the daily stress of schools and teenagers or husbands' betrayals. And it will be years before we realize, during the great shift that is yet to come, what we have missed. Essentially, we've done as we've pleased and, despite financial worries and job dissatisfaction, with the aid of regular exercise and good bras, we've made it to older age with the kind of physical agility and joyful wonder many people associate with youth.

Lily has not fared so well, and upon seeing her bony old woman face with cheekbones so prominent they resemble tumors, the lines carving the sides of her wilted mouth, and her new glasses that are so thick it's like looking through the wrong end of a telescope at her eyeballs, Leslie and I freeze.

"Come in," she says. "Hi, Maya. Hi, Spud. Oh, it's so nice to have dogs here again."

As she turns to show us into her parlor, Leslie glances at me. I glance at the back of Lily's white wispy-haired head and see straight through to pink scalp, I open my mouth in barely exaggerated horror, then shake my head to Leslie to keep quiet.

"I'm sure they smell Wilma everywhere," continues Lily disconsolately. "I understand death has a distinctive stink. Coffee? Tea? Water?"

"Wow!" says Leslie, taking in the parlor furniture and warm colors.

"Oh, that's right, you've never been here," replies Lily. "Betsy has, but— What would you both like to drink?'

"Nothing for me, thanks," I answer.

"Leslie?"

"This is beautiful, Lily," says Leslie, drifting to the Chagall print. "Is this real?"

"No, no, just a print. Just a fantasy. Coffee?"

"No thanks," says Leslie, mesmerized and moving to within an inch of "The Birthday." "I drank coffee with breakfast."

"So!" I announce, trying to inject focus through our mutual fog. "Edith's Ouija board! Where should I put it?"

"Edith?" asks Lily, sounding alarmed.

"How about the dogs?" asks Leslie.

"Pardon?" says Lily.

"Something to drink for the dogs?" asks Leslie.

"Oh," says Lily, distracted. "Water's in the kitchen. I still have Wilma's bowls. You didn't tell me the board belonged to somebody named Edith. I don't like that name."

"Lily, relax," I say, hoping this doesn't make her tense up even more, and predictably it does.

"I just don't like the name. It sounds mean. Now do you want something to drink or not?"

"You're a great hostess," I say, adopting what I hope is a comforting and maternal tone. "But we're your friends. You don't have to take care of us. You look like you haven't slept in a month."

Lily takes off her glasses and wipes them on the corner of a sleeve that belongs in a recycle ragbag. Shifting her weight onto her bare right foot, I see a posture reminiscent of the awkward teenager she must have been.

"What can we do to help?" I ask.

Taking the cue, Leslie unleashes both dogs, clears the coffee table, and sets up the Ouija board. I race to the kitchen, put down a water bowl, call the dogs, and am back in the parlor in less than a minute.

"Let's sit here, Lily," directs Leslie. "Betsy, move that chair over here, will you?"

And together, Leslie and I do our best to take care of Lily, who rocks vacantly from one long, spindly, baggy-panted leg to the other, blind, her glasses dangling from her right thumb and pointer finger, her long wormy toes curling into the Persian carpet as if desperately looking for an opening.

I suppose I should have given some thought to what we would ask the Ouija board, but honestly I didn't care. My main interest was getting together and making sure Lily was alive.

"Is anybody there?" I intone, feeling ridiculous as Leslie, Lily, and I rest our fingers lightly on the plastic planchette. And I think we are all a bit surprised when the thing suddenly springs to life, madly circling the board. "You two are doing that, right?" I say.

"No," say Leslie and Lily, earnestly shaking their heads. Maya barks at Spud, and the two dogs begin a game of chase and wrestle until Spud is trapped under the coffee table and Maya, in a play bow, yaps from under Leslie's feet.

The planchette whips our hands from *E* to *N* to *J*. "Enjoy?" asks Lily and the planchette zips to "yes," as if sliding into home base. Briefly it pauses and then resumes jumping around the alphabet—

"I better write this down," says Leslie, starting to remove her fingers.

"No!" Lily and I shout.

"I'll remember," says Lily, whose blue eyes now resemble pin lights shooting through the fog of her thick lenses, tracking the planchette as it whips around the board.

"Enjoy Exotic Zoo," Lily marvels when it is finished—making lazy circles around "Goodbye" at the bottom of the board.

"What kind of message is that?" asks Leslie.

"The dogs," I answer. "The dogs and us. The zoo. We're supposed to enjoy it."

"Oh," says Leslie, impressed by either my powers of interpretation or the fact that anything at all happened or simply glad that it is over because of her Trumpian attention span. "Well, that was interesting." And she wipes her hands and tells Maya to hush, even though she's no longer barking at Spud.

"So, you're still working for Bernie Sanders?" Lily asks Leslie, no doubt picking up my Trump thought with her magic psychic powers. "He's not going to win. You're wasting your time."

"Excuse me?" says Leslie.

"Forgive me," says Lily, putting her bony hand to her forehead. "I have allergies and I hate the name Edith. Plus missing Wilma. I'm not myself. I'm sure you're doing a great thing by being a political activist."

Leslie and I exchange a look, fully aware that it is not private because no matter how clogged Lily is, she misses nothing. Nor do Leslie and I. As I said, we are married. One entity. Hard to explain.

"I think you should get out of your apartment, like right now, Lily," I suggest helpfully. "Put on some shoes and let's all enjoy some more exotic zoo in Central Park. Have you even seen a tree since Wilma died? You look like a bag lady."

Without conferring with one another, we let Maya and Spud lead the walk, and I remember how comfortable our park threesome used to be.

East on Seventy-fourth, south on Central Park West, into the park at Seventy-second, past the beggar with the guitar who's never learned to play and the souvenir buttons and John Lennon photos stand, across the street to Strawberry Fields, swerving south to avoid the tourists snapping selfies on the flower-covered sidewalk "Imagine" mosaic, weaving effortlessly. As older women, we are invisible, one of the benefits of age. Through the panhandlers, drug addicts, and hucksters, we head down the south hill and out across West Drive. I assume we are going to continue east past the Daniel Webster statue, but Maya says no, and without chatter, we head due north and stroll in comfortable silence all the way up to the Great Lawn.

"The tourists weren't too bad," comments Leslie as we turn en masse onto the path due east, past the Delacorte Theater, past the Romeo & Juliet and Tempest statues, then north around the Great Lawn.

"I guess not," I answer. "But why do they crowd like that around the mosaic? It's a bunch of stones for goodness sake."

"I'm sorry," huffs Lily, "but I do not enjoy this exotic zoo!"

Leslie and I laugh, but Lily's face is stone.

"Care to elaborate?" I ask.

And so begins Lily's quiet, sensible, relentless tirade about her loathing of herds, herd movements, herd competition, and how perhaps if she were a wild dog she'd feel differently, but she simply cannot enjoy people acting without personal discernment and thinking.

"Are you finished?" asks Leslie, as we turn east on the Great Lawn loop and head in the direction of the Metropolitan Museum.

"As a matter of fact, no," replies Lily, and Leslie rolls her eyes at me.

"Don't roll your eyes, Leslie, this is serious!" snaps Lily without even turning her head toward Leslie. "Remember what happened to my boss when we were at the museum?" And although none of us could ever forget the Black versus White debacle, Lily proceeds to recount the whole thing.

"And the worst," she finally concludes, "the absolute worst was I'm absolutely certain my boss had some kind of face blindness—that's a real thing now you know; it's been diagnosed; I saw it on a news program—as well as multiple learning problems; she could not spell to save her life. And it had nothing to do with racism! But the herd moved and she got stampeded out of there because it was politically correct to assume she was a racist and everybody was too busy enjoying being self-righteously angry to even think there might be another explanation."

Leslie reddens, and when she speaks, her voice is stiff in a way I don't associate with her rubbery personality. "I remember it, Lily. But I also understand it. I work with inner-city kids now, and if you had any idea what they face just walking into a room—"

But Lily won't hear it. She flips up her hand dismissively in Leslie's direction and scoffs. "People are individuals, not a herd! I'm sure anybody looking at the three of us could make a million assumptions about our privilege and our place in society—

Leslie goes rigid. "So you agree with Trump about political correctness?"

"I don't agree with Trump or anybody!" declares Lily. "I'm just saying herd movements are not always right. People need to think! That's the only way to stop what's—"

Silence. She doesn't finish the thought and we don't ask.

More silence. But we keep walking.

"My ex-husband told me I'm aloof," says Lily finally. "And you two are just as aloof as I am."

At the eastern limit of the northern Great Lawn loop, we have a choice: north to the Reservoir, east to the Metropolitan Museum, or south past the browning cherry trees to finish the circle or continue south to the Ramble. Nobody—neither dogs nor humans—is willing to take responsibility for a decision, so instead we sit on a bench in front of the playground.

"What does your ex-husband do anyway?" asks Leslie, who has taken the high road regarding the political correctness dispute. "You never told us anything about him."

"Something to do with table tennis," says Lily dryly. "He writes commercials about small balls."

We laugh. Thank goodness, Lily is lightening up.

"And by the way, it turns out we're still married."

Maya leaps off my lap after a squirrel. Spud follows her. We watch after the dogs, keeping an eye out for park gestapo because it's after nine a.m. and leash law flaunting now costs $150.

"Do you feel like a loser?" asks Leslie, directing it into the air.

I do, but I don't answer.

"Why do you ask?" asks Lily suspiciously.

"Well, you're talking about herds and hating that life's a competition, and if you feel like a loser, it means you're part of the herd, competing just like everybody else—or else why would you feel that you're losing?"

"I'm impressed," I say into the air.

"If you feel like a loser," continues Leslie, "there is a possibility that you're suffering from Anosognosia."

"Gesundheit," I reply.

"Anosognosia—the psychiatric term for lack of awareness of one's own condition." Leslie shoots me an "I dare you" look. "I read books too."

"I'll do a rewrite."

Leslie laughs and calls Spud, so I call Maya. We walk south following Maya, knowing that somebody is going to have to make a decision about which way to turn when we get past the cherry trees.

"How did you feel when you used to get messages?" I ask Lily suddenly.

"What do you mean?"

"Like in your body—when you knew something psychic for a client. How did it feel?"

Lily stops, seems to inventory her torso without moving. "Soft, I guess. In here." And she points to her chest.

"So you weren't scared?"

"No," she answers. "Why would I be?"

"I don't know."

"But you weren't friends with your clients," offers Leslie, and I wonder if I have completely miswritten her and she's some kind of savant.

"Of course not," says Lily. "They paid me. The end."

"How'd you feel when they paid you?" continues Leslie, and I accept that I've handed her the conversation baton.

"I don't know," says Lily, beginning to get impatient. "How should I feel? Money is nice. I was glad to have it."

"But you didn't feel soft?" I say and Leslie gives me a dirty look—she's got this.

I shut up and wait.

"You didn't feel soft toward your clients?" says Leslie.

"No," says Lily, sounding a little surprised. "I barely knew them."

"So," says Leslie, breathing as if she is about to lift a three hundred-pound weight, "so if you *had* felt soft, how would that have been?"

"Ludicrous," snaps Lily without a pause to think.

"Why?" ask Leslie and I as one, and she accepts my assist.

"Maybe you feel like *you* when you feel hard," I almost whisper, unsure if I'm prompting Leslie or Lily or playing Spectator for all three of us. But there is no need for worry because there is absolutely no resistance from Lily.

"Of course I'm me when I'm hard. That's who I am. I go my own way. You have to be hard to be on your own, to buck the unthinking herd."

"But why?" asks Leslie, almost plaintively, and Lily's mouth drops open.

"Maybe you're afraid you can't be you if you feel soft around people," I suggest. "That you'll get lost in the human herd. Because we're *all* herd animals—even if we refuse to move. That's still a herd choice because it affects everybody who runs you over, stops, or changes direction to avoid collision. You're still part of it. There is no other option. Like Leslie said, maybe you're unaware of your true condition. And maybe it would be better to at least see it. Which you can't if you're so hard all the time."

And to my astonishment, Lily freezes, closes her eyes, takes a giant breath of new mulch and cut-grass-infused air, then lets it out slowly, seeming to track it from her lungs and stomach, up her throat, and out through her mouth.

Leslie mouths to me, "Anosognosia." And we wait.

Lily opens her eyes, first staring at the pavement and then slowly raises her face, tracking Leslie and me, from our feet, up our legs, over our torsos, to our eyes. We have stopped breathing, so I shove Leslie. We both breathe and return Lily's gaze. And like a slow motion movie, we watch her eyes fill with tears, then widen in abject terror.

"No!" she declares, and marches forward with Leslie and me hustling to keep up.

When we get to the south end where the loop turns west back to the Delacorte or east to the museum, or east and then south to the Ramble, I make the decision to extend this walk. "The Ramble," I pronounce, and Leslie and Lily don't argue.

"So let me get this straight," says Leslie, after we've entered the north meadow of the woodland, and seem to be heading back west toward home, bypassing the actual woods, "it's too scary to be soft around people because you don't think you can be you, a spectator who is not part of a herd, even though the herd is a given. And you're upset about how the herd acts and that you can't change it, so life is not perfect, and because it's not, you're sitting it out."

Lily doesn't answer, so I do. "Yup, that pretty much sums things up for me."

And all three of us laugh.

"Trogloxenes," says Leslie.

"Come again?" I answer. I am going to have to do a complete revision of *Plan Z by Leslie Kove.*

"Trogloxenes. Animals that live underground or just inside caves—they come and go because they can't stand staying in either place. Or in vernacular, self-righteous irritating pompous prigs who always tell the truth as they see it."

A breeze ruffles the upper reaches of the massive black tupelo tree—planted by Frederick Law Olmstead in 1862—the centerpiece of the north field, spreading her boughs like a many-armed Great Mother welcoming her children to rest. We look up and that's when we notice the hawk. It's sitting in the crook of two of the lower branches. And right beneath it, staring unblinking and appearing almost sanguine, a pigeon. One is the hunter, the other the prey. Both clear-eyed and soft.

In such a low voice she is almost inaudible, Lily says, "What if you see something, know something, so awful, so devastating, what if you see such destruction on the way that it will end things as we know them, and there is nothing you can do about it, because of the herds?"

"Maybe just watch it softly," I answer. "Maybe just that can help."

CHAPTER 25

Lily invents a new morning ablution. While she brushes her teeth, she stares in the mirror, but not at her teeth as she is accustomed. Instead, breathing deeply and slowly through both her nose and mouth, around the electric tooth brush, she gazes into her own eyes, willing herself to be soft. Her eyeglasses are a problem so she removes them, and even though her reflection is now a flesh-colored blur with a white hair halo, she attempts to relax her eyeballs. After several weeks of this, she realizes that relaxing her eyeballs seems to make the back of her head—her occipital region—expand. Which in turn, makes her neck softer and her arms feel like spaghetti. This results in so much drooled toothpaste that she takes to removing her nightgown and brushing nude.

Like the connection of her uterus point to full-body orgasms, she realizes soft eyes are wired to manual dexterity, and to develop her abilities, she begins to brush her teeth with her nondominant left hand while doing biceps curls with her right arm.

With her eyeglasses on, she practices looking softly into her morning coffee while stirring counterclockwise with her left hand.

Each of these practices she notes clearly in her diary, tracking her progress, varying the sequences to see if it makes a difference.

After several weeks of rigorous soft-eye training, Lily decides that it is time to test her soft-eye visual acuity and tolerance on other humans—to determine if she can remain herself while being soft with other members of the human herd. Her first attempt is from a bench at the entrance to Central Park at Seventy-second Street—where she quickly learns, from the leers of several men and the dirty looks of many women, that this is not a good idea.

Next are the checkout clerks at Fairway—ineffective since they do not look at anyone but each other. She tries at the library checkout. Same thing. So although she has lived in her neighborhood for more than forty years, she decides to query passersby for directions.

"Can you tell me where the nearest subway station is?" she asks a soft-looking middle-aged woman in blue jeans and a paisley blouse on Columbus Avenue—the first pedestrian she's seen who is not on a cell phone.

"Where would you like to go, dear?" asks the woman, looking at her so gently that Lily feels their eyes merge—which causes Lily's adrenal glands to spurt and her heart to jolt, and certain that she is having a heart attack, Lily gasps, "Never mind. Sorry to bother— I'm out of sequence," as she flees north.

By the time she gets home, her heart has stopped pounding, but she is still panting—desperate little breaths holding back what feels like a flood behind her eyes—a flood that breaks the breath dyke as soon as she's inside her apartment, locking the door behind her.

And she sobs, with no idea what frightened her so or why she is crying. And that's when the vision comes. The same vision she had at the Spectators' Club so many years ago, the same one that started playing in her dreams like a catastrophic poem of images a few months ago, the same one she's kept at bay most of her adult life. And she knows unequivocally that if she softens her eyes, she will merge with everyone, and then it will feel worse if it happens.

"It was a panic attack," Leslie explains when she calls to inquire about using Lily's parlor for an inner-city kids' event. "I used to get them all the time, but now hardly ever."

"What if it happens with your kids?" Lily almost whispers. "Is Betsy coming too?"

"I think so. She said she'd come if you do, and if we're doing it at your place—"

Lily is angry at herself. Angry that she is stuck. "All right," she says to Leslie. "Lord knows, Bernie Madoff was in my parlor. Maybe this will balance things."

Leslie is puzzled but doesn't want to push her luck. Best to lock this in and end the conversation. "Okay. You don't have to do anything but greet people and be White."

Lily laughs.

"The kids are mostly Black and Hispanic and the point is to introduce them to chatting with White people, which they'll have to do at fundraisers for our organization where they'll make contacts which will lead to job interviews, so you qualify even though you're not a corporate type; a couple of those will be there as well, and the group leader and I will come early with refreshments. Thank you sooo much, Lily. You have no idea how helpful this is. See you in three weeks."

For three weeks, Lily cleans the whole apartment, but mainly the parlor, the kitchen, and the little bathroom downstairs. And while she cleans, she listens to news shows on the radio. She listens furiously, determined to connect to her culture. She listens fiercely with a dull background sense that time is running out, but she never articulates that. When she's tired of cleaning, she reads news—on Facebook, clicking on so many articles in the *Washington Post* and the *New York Times* that she quickly reaches her allowable quota of freebies, so then she subscribes to the digital *Times*. Even though she has no formal education to speak of, it is important to be an informed White person in case any of the inner-city children want to discuss politics and social issues. Leslie certainly seems to know what's going on, and Betsy doesn't say much, but she usually agrees with Leslie about the latest political controversies, so chances are she stays afloat in the sea of current events.

The Wednesday before the Inner-city Kids' Talking to White People Practice event, a young White man walks into a Black church in Charleston, South Carolina, and assassinates nine worshipers. Friday, the twenty-one-year-old killer is arrested and he declares that he did it in order to start a race war and Lily can't sleep.

By the time Leslie and the perky young workshop leader, Giselle, arrive the next afternoon with boxes of soft drinks and platters of cut vegetables and dip, Lily has been awake for approximately two days and has attempted to refresh herself by repeatedly slapping cold water on her face and neck.

"Hi," bubbles Giselle.

She has dimples, a square jaw, short-cropped jerry curls, and perfect light brown skin. Lily attempts to look soft-eyed, but mostly she is trying to remain upright.

"I'm Giselle Hernandez," says the girl, making direct eye contact, putting down her boxes, and extending her right hand.

"Lily Hogue," says Lily, wiping her wet hand on her pants and then shaking Giselle's. "Welcome. I hope the parlor is clean enough. Right in there."

Giselle flicks Leslie a questioning look, then picks up her boxes and cheerfully marches into the parlor, as directed by Lily's frozen traffic-cop arm pointing due left.

"What can I do?" asks Lily as Leslie and Giselle fall into a well-choreographed and rehearsed dance of setting up.

"Nothing," say Giselle and Leslie.

"Don't worry," says Leslie, clearing the coffee table as Giselle unloads plastic cups and drinks onto Mrs. S's antique sideboard. "You did plenty by providing the space. When people come, you can answer the door. Just look them in the eyes and let them shake your hand."

Lily gulps, leans against a wall, and wonders what to do with her hands. If only Wilma were still alive. Wilma made things easier. If only she had thought to suggest that Leslie bring Spud and Betsy bring Maya. *Buzz, buzz.*

"Lily, you're on," says Leslie. "That's probably Betsy. You don't have to shake her hand."

Lily buzzes the front door open, and I come in.

"How do you do?" I say, thinking I'm making a joke. "Betsy Robinson. Pleased to meet you." And I extend my hand.

Lily grabs it in what feels like an icy death grip. "You didn't bring Maya," she gasps.

"Too many big feet for little dogs," I say. "Relax, Lily. Breathe, okay? Like this?" And I demonstrate.

"Okay," whispers Lily. "I'm sorry. I haven't slept since the shooting."

"It's going to be all right," I say in my calmest professional editor's voice, knowing exactly what she is talking about, because, even though I'm on a very early draft at this point, I wrote this. "You're having a panic attack. I know all about this. I've had plenty of them, and so has Leslie. You're not nuts. You just need to breathe. Now move out of the way so I can bring in more party shit."

Lily does not pass out. She goes upstairs to her bedroom, combs her wispy hair, puts on real shoes and lipstick, and when the intercom buzzes, greets all the kids and corporate types as they enter the apartment. Everybody is on time, as they have been warned that this is a one-hour event and being on time is part of professional behavior. Giselle, the perky event leader, is a cheerleader, and rather than allow anybody to feel a second of party discomfort, immediately announces the first exercise: In a circle around the parlor, each White adult will be paired with a group of three or four kids, all of whom have recently concluded internships at some of the corporations recruited for the program by the wealthy board members, and they will discuss their favorite color. The exercise is to give the kids the experience that conversation about anything is possible and can be easy with strangers: Party chatter 101. And as Lily, Leslie, and I begin, it occurs to all of us that perhaps we will benefit from this exercise as much or even more than the kids.

For the second exercise, the groups of kids rotate to the next White adult and this time we are to again introduce ourselves and then discuss work experiences. Lily's kids are a short, overweight Hispanic boy with ill-fitted glasses even thicker than Lily's that are precariously balanced halfway down his wide nose, an elegant Black girl in a green knit dress with a violet scarf who looks as if she should be teaching this workshop or sitting on a corporate board already, and a large Black girl with a nearly shaved head, a tattoo snaking around her neck, giant hoop earrings, and a "Don't mess with me" expression on her heavily made-up face.

"So," says Lily, taking a deep breath and letting it out slowly. "Lily Hogue is my name." In the last exercise, the kids were spontaneous about their love of red and black and distaste for blue, and all she'd had to do was ask the question. "So?" she asks this time, and nobody answers. "Well," she begins, "I'm not really a role model in that I haven't had corporate jobs, so I'd love to know what you've experienced in your internships."

The three kids feel like a wall. A concrete wall.

"So how about you?" says Lily, directing a determined smile at the girl with the hoop earrings. "What's your name and where did you work and how did you feel about it?"

"What I wanna know," says the girl, making direct unblinking eye contact, "is if you never worked for no corporation an' you just born rich, how you supposed to help us?"

Lily feels her legs wilt, but before they collapse, the other two kids step forward.

"Hey," says the boy, "chill, Denise. Easy, huh?" And then to Lily, "Her name's Denise and she think she tough. I'm Cory."

Denise shifts her weight to the other foot, stares at the floor, and plays with one hoop earring.

"I worked at a law firm," offers the elegant girl in carefully articulated syllables. "I'm Kiana. It was very stressful because I had to learn lots of new rules and stuff, but I was fine."

"Talk like yourself, why don't you?" snaps Denise.

"Denise!" protests Kiana.

Cory raises his hand and from seemingly out of nowhere, Giselle appears, affably stepping between Denise and Kiana. "So how are we all doing here? Denise? Are you having some problems?"

Denise stares at the floor and mumbles, "Nothin' wrong here, Giselle," landing hard on the two syllables of Giselle's name.

"How about if Denise and I take a little break," suggests Giselle, guiding away Denise, who transforms into a petulant ten-year-old, rolling her eyes to the ceiling."

"She think she tough is all," says Cory, attempting a mediating smile.

"My first day at the law firm, I was so scared, I had to run to the ladies' about twenty times," says Kiana, and Lily and she lock soft eyes.

And that is the moment it hits. It slices Lily's heart as if it is the real knife that will soon end the girl's life, and Lily knows, and before she can stop the knowing and the feelings, the tears overbrim and run down her face beneath her eyeglasses, and without thinking, she seizes Kiana's skinny wrist and Kiana is pulling back, terrified, and Cory's hand shoots up like a salute and this time it's Leslie who comes over, and seeing what is happening, and understanding because she too has grappled with trauma and PTSD and inappropriate responses and because Leslie and Lily and dead Harmony and lost Zelda and I, Betsy, are all the same person, she softly peels Lily's fingers off Kiana's strangled wrist and signals to Giselle, who almost telepathically understands and ends the exercise.

Shaken and trembling, Lily withdraws, apologizes to Kiana, saying that she has not been feeling well since the death of her dog and has not slept since the attack of the worshippers in Charlottesville, and excusing herself, she bids us good-bye and tells us to enjoy the parlor and take as long as we want, just to lock the door when we're done.

Giselle is perplexed, but ever the improviser, uses the moment for teaching and, for our last exercise, tells us to imagine that we've just come from a shocking event—a car accident, witnessing a shooting, whatever, and feel free to take it from real life—and we're thrown into a professional situation. Do we mention what's happened or pretend everything is fine?

Most people choose to pretend.

This is followed by fifteen minutes of undirected mingling when all the Black and Hispanic kids ignore the Whites and gather around the refreshments. Then Giselle thanks all the White people and corporate types for helping the kids, and she and the kids applaud them. The kids form a receiving line to the door and, as they exit, the corporate types give out business cards.

Leslie, Giselle, and I clean up, and I stay to check on Lily.

Through her bedroom door, Lily yells that she is fine and to go home; she doesn't feel like talking. So I do.

For the next couple of days, Leslie tells me, Lily calls her—morning and night—begging for Kiana's phone number, pleading that she knows it sounds insane, but she has to warn her.

"Warn her to do what?" Leslie asks me. "Stop using the subway? Stop living? Hide?"

"Do you think she's snapped?" I ask.

"Maybe. Or what if she's right and something is going to happen to Kiana?"

On June 24, four days after our event, Dzhokhar Tsarnaev, the Boston

Marathon bomber, is sentenced to death and Kiana is stabbed to death by her uncle.

"Do you think I should call Lily?" Leslie asks me.

I don't answer. Partly because I don't know the answer, but also because, even as I am writing this, I believe in free will for all characters.

"I think I should call her," she says. "It's the right thing to do."

CHAPTER 26

How far back did the disconnection and spectating begin?

There was the generation that came of age in the eighteenth century: herds of immigrants, Lily's great grandparents—Polish and Russian Jews in Mrs. Hogue's line, a root that was violently severed due to her great grandparents' fierce desire to flee the motherland, forget the pogroms, and quickly assimilate into a new country. That, combined with her great grandmother's Aryan good looks, passed on to her daughter and then to Mrs. Hogue—let's call her Madeline—ensured that by the time Madeline bore her own children, she never even thought to mention the lineage.

But despite ignorance of the violent root-severing, what continued through the DNA—from the great grandparents and further back from the herds of wandering exiled Jews—was a history of desperation and flight: overbearing, yet absent, laboring fathers, barely able to breathe, strangled by the belief that although they didn't speak the language of whatever new country they'd fled to, their mandate went beyond making good; they must become rich so that they could provide for the wives whom they both desired and resented. And who were the wives, but all those self-effacing mothers whose very life depended on marriage to resentful men who had been spoiled by mothers who instilled in them a sense of entitlement while dominating and emasculating them with expectations that they could never meet.

Post-Depression and World War II, the daughters of these couples developed into women like Madeline whose role required self-erasure in order to serve as mothers and lovers to ever more demanding, resentful, insecure husbands. Add to this tangle that in the early nineteenth century, men like Madeline's father with conflicted sexuality—who later found their soulmates in men servants like the Sal of Madeline Hogue's story to Lily—believed their degenerate proclivity was best ignored and denied, and thus it fueled more absence and resentment.

So in 1947, when Madeline married Rudolph Hogue—newly home from Korea, whose life's momentum had been shattered by the bombing of Nagasaki and the pre-war draft, who was the son of an overworked upholsterer and his mousy subservient wife who derived from French Jews and Polish immigrants much like Madeline's ancestors—parents disdained and rejected by Rudy for their lack of sophistication and taste—the binding glue was not love, but a complete lack of ancestral roots combined with a loathing of any herd movement that was not of their own choosing and infatuation based on their agreement about the saintliness of their mothers and the inadequacy of their fathers as well as a mutual desire to flee Oklahoma and create their own autonomous herd.

Marriage in New York's Westchester County suburbs quickly led to a habit of nightly, then daily, then hourly drinking—port for her; Scotch for him—and of course smoking, as all young couples did in the late 1940s. The night that Lily was conceived, Madeline was exhausted after birthing two babies in two years. It wasn't exactly rape; it was more that she allowed herself to be used even though she had clearly said no. She rationalized what happened, as her mother and many women before her had done, with the belief that, like laundry and cooking, sex was her duty.

Without intent or foreplay, Rudy Hogue pinned his wife open in a splayed position, pumped his buttocks, and blitzkrieged her vagina with sperm, millions of which bombarded the vicinity, releasing an electrical storm of hyaluronidase, dissolving the protective coating of an ovum and eliminating all defenses for a single mucous homing missile to impale the just-released egg hiding in the nether region of Madeline's left fallopian tube. On contact, it pinned the egg, squashing their nuclei into one Lily Hogue zygote, which glided down the tube until it was floating freely in Madeline's uterus where it began dividing. Miraculously, this clump of Lily survived a tidal wave of douche fluid the next morning, paroxysms of weeping, and torrents of toxins as Madeline drowned her dread of another baby in port. Embedding firmly in Madeline's endometrium, multi-celled Lily hung on for dear life through more douche deluges, the probing of gloved fingers, then a freezing speculum. Exhausted, she bunkered, vibrating and pulsating with life, merging tissues with Madeline, despite her mother's desperation to be rid of her.

There were no soothing lullabies or tummy caresses. Through Madeline's willful darkness and even occasional "accidental" combative full-frontal bumps, Lily entrenched, rooting into the blood-rich womb, enduring tsunamis of alcohol and nicotine, floods of stress hormone, and when in December of 1950, Madeline's mother died, a siege of quaking, shaking, and trembling as her mother's toxic defenders tried to evict Lily. Grief-stricken and furious at being left by her own mother, Madeline couldn't eat and attempted to starve herself and the unborn baby, but still Lily held on and grew.

And on February 14, 1951, the normal distress tremors and assaults gave way to a new kind of squeezing, swaying, undulating, and pushing that quickly turned into a formidable downward suck, and in one volcanic eruption, baby Lily was finally expelled into her premier headfirst dive.

Despite her harrowing journey in utero, baby Lily did what all little ones do: she searched for connection in loving eyes, only to discover the fierce, starving orbs of a terrified animal, desperate to flee a trap. To such an animal, feeding does not come easily, so nurturance, too, became a battle between mother and baby; Lily, who could not protest in any other way, turned away from the milk of her mother's icy breast.

Formula, the doctor directed, and choosing between starvation and life, miraculously Lily chose the bottle; its liquid was sweet and creamy. She sucked with gusto.

After Madeline's rough tummy-scrubbing mistake and the bloodied umbilicus, baby Lily stopped squealing or grunting or making any of the sounds babies do to communicate with their mothers. And as Lily's broken stump healed, it gave off a horrible rotting odor further repelling Madeline—reminding her of what she had done—so Madeline was relieved when it finally dropped off. Never again would she touch that place. Let it gather dirt. And so the wounds from mother to child had been delivered: poison feedings, a stab to Lily's baby heart, acid in her expectant newborn eyes, a navel rape—quick training to avoid contact, let alone the eye-to-eye mergence that is key to sociality and survival. Where Lily's baby heart should be, there opened what felt like a gaping hole: a profound vacuum, loss, a canyon-size ache, a never-ending falling backwards through nothing. And in that nothing was a heavy void. And as Lily grew, it too grew—to the size of an elephant weighing on Lily's child-size psyche, engendering sadness that made it hard to cry. And so young Lily learned to watch. She became an expert spectator—as hypersensitive to the movements and needs of others as were her unknown ancestors who stealthily escaped the purges and pogroms and fled across the sea to a foreign land. And true to her unknown lineage, desperately she survived.

After the news of Kiana's death, Lily cannot get out of bed. She hardly knew the girl. Yet this is what she feels: a savage pain all over, a profound vacuum, a loss, a canyon-size ache, a never-ending falling backwards through nothing. Lying in bed, she glances at her reflection in the closet door mirror, and never having seen any aged relatives because they never lived that long, she doesn't know what to make of the wizened Jew looking back at her. Sighing and looking away—she must either take down that mirror or cover it with something—she gives in to the elephant weight that has always been there, and in an odd way, it feels good.

CHAPTER 27

Eventually Lily does get out of bed. She returns to errands and the business of daily life. She reads library books, considers adopting another dog but doesn't, and all the while she flinches at an impending sense of infiltration.

"Infiltration?" asks Leslie. "What does that mean?"

We—Leslie and I (Betsy)—are . . .

A brief writer's tangent: Where are we and what we are doing? I haven't a clue. The reason for this next scene is that we—Leslie and I and perhaps Lily as well—are concerned about Lily since Kiana died, because Lily seems to feel responsible and worthless. But that is only partly true. The whole truth is that I need my spectator friends as much as they need me. I claim to have written them, so I must contain them, but this is not exactly true. They contain me as much as I do them. And who contains all of us? Who or what writes me writing them? What etheric umbilical cord conveys all that is? A birthing is happening, but who is birthing what? These are questions that drive me crazy, and the only people who would even listen to me talk about this without directing me post-haste to a therapist or an ashram are other spectators. We are a tribe. And since I don't know all the answers and rely on free will, I'm hoping Leslie or Lily will provide some insight. Or at least a location for the next scene.

Okay, back to the story: Leslie has just asked what I mean by saying Lily has an impending dread of infiltration.

"Infiltration—into all of our systems, poised to send them into chaos," I say dryly. "Lily told me she has nightmares about it. And for a while she couldn't get out of bed. I've been having crummy dreams too? How about you?"

"Yup."

"Well, in that case, do you think we should get together?"

Leslie and I are on the phone, and, since I haven't written beyond this point, I am hoping she will quickly supply the venue and activity for our next meeting.

She doesn't answer, but I hear chewing. "Are you eating a carrot?"

"I resonate with this 'dread of infiltration.' Probably we *should* get together," she says.

I wait for a venue.

Leslie chews. "It's too hot," she finally mumbles. "And I hate Trump and the sound of my air conditioner. This place is so tiny it feels like I'm living inside the thing. I'd like to move, but it's too hot to think. Also, I hate my job and I can't quit because who the hell would hire a woman in her sixties, and a couple more years and I get a package and I can move out of this matchbox. Trump sounds worse than my air conditioner. He makes my hair follicles hurt. I cannot believe that asshole is going to run for president. I hate him, I hate him, I hate him."

We decide to call Lily—*I* will call her—and meet on the bench opposite the waterfall in the Hallett Nature Sanctuary at the southernmost end of park next to the Pond. We have never been inside the Sanctuary because it's closed unless you go on a no-dogs-allowed Central Park Conservancy-sponsored tour, and, because we are self-righteous, irritating, pompous prigs, we reject that. But the bench opposite the waterfall is always at least ten degrees cooler than the rest of New York City, plus we like the sound of the water crashing down from a cliff. Nine thirty a.m. is rendezvous time: Me and Maya, Leslie and Spud, and Lily in whatever shape she is in. It's almost a month since the kids' event in Lily's parlor and we don't know what to expect.

"I brought brunch," I say, and Lily and Leslie look skeptical. None of us are cooks or terribly knowledgeable about food except that we enjoy eating what we want—large amounts of a select few foods, which we consume over and over again, like dogs—and we have a long list of things we don't touch which makes us pariahs in the eyes of foodies and hyper-judgmental eaters who are often overweight and want everybody to eat the only "right way" which is indiscriminately and full of sugar.

"Vegan bacon and a double-order of fluffy soy eggs with garlic and peppers for Leslie and me," I say, offering Leslie a take-out container. "No bread." None of us eat the stuff; Leslie and I were once overweight and learned to stay away from addictive white flour and sugar. "But whole-grain organic cereal with blackberries for Lily. Here's the almond milk."

"Spoon?" asks Lily, and knowing how much she dislikes putting plastic in her mouth, I produce a stainless steel utensil from my vast and varied collection of cutlery from hotels all over the country from the days when I was a touring actress (another story).

"Wow," she sighs, inhaling the fresh oats as if tasting through her nostrils, which flare and quiver with enjoyment.

"And a selection of fruit!" I announce, presenting a bag of organic strawberries, bananas, oranges (even though Lily's teeth are too sensitive for acidic produce), and a small juicy cantaloupe cut in perfect thirds which was no small feat. "Berries washed in filtered water, a side of yellow quinoa with crunchy French-cut string beans, and—*duh-dada-dah*—a chaser of greasy home fries to coat our arteries and let us die happy."

"Gold star," grunts Leslie, digging into her scrambled fake eggs with a standard take-out plastic spoon.

"If it had been dinner, I would have brought broccoli," I add, just to prove that I know us well, and we all make *yum* sounds as we dig into brunch.

"This was very nice of you," says Leslie.

"I know."

"Do you want money?" asks Lily through a mouthful of oats.

"Always," I answer, "but not for this." I laugh. Nobody else does. And we all chew enthusiastically, enjoying the tastes with the moist wind from the splashing, crashing waterfall and the sound of quacking ducks over the background roar of Fifty-ninth Street traffic.

"Turtle," says Leslie, gesturing at the Pond bank with her fork.

Maya and Spud take refuge under our bench, lying flat on the cool wet pavement.

"So, Lily, do you still feel like shit about Kiana?" I query.

Lily eyes me, squinting through her lenses, then decides to lie. "I didn't know the girl. I wanted to warn her, but no, I don't feel like shit. Leslie was right. I would have sounded insane if I had called her. I'm absolutely fine. Perfect. This is very good oatmeal."

As the turtle plops back into the water, the great white heron that usually hunts from the tree limbs overhanging the water on east side of the Pond, away from walking paths and the cell-phone-clicking tourists, lights on the rock incline to the right of the waterfall. He ignores us but we can feel him observing.

"Sorry, buddy, no fish here," mumbles Leslie without looking up from her eggs.

"Well, I'm upset about it," I say, finishing my eggs and staring into my lap. "I'm upset that girl was killed. I'm upset that Lily slipped into another so-called time slice and felt it and couldn't do anything about it. I'm upset that I know things all the time that I can't tell anybody without sounding insane. I'm upset that it's never something useful like a lottery number and I'm upset that Trump is going to win the election and there is not a damn thing we can do about it."

Lily drops her cereal spoon and it *pings* on the pavement, bouncing under our bench, scaring the dogs; Leslie chokes on her quinoa; and the air around us whooshes out in concentric waves—as if an energetic boulder just dropped from the sky, leaving in its wake a vacuum. It only lasts a couple of seconds, but we all feel it and can't breathe.

"The truth is, I'm lonely," I finally say, and as the great white heron takes off for the other side of the Pond, Lily and Leslie don't answer.

Despite what we all know, Leslie works tirelessly for Bernie Sanders. She reminds Lily that she (Lily) is the one that told her (Leslie) that her brother Peter wants her to keep trying. Neither Lily nor I can argue with the sanity of this, so I do a bit for Bernie too—with the understanding that he'll never win and I'll support Hillary Clinton when she gets the nomination. Lily is immobile and will not talk about it. If we ask, she says it's her dreams. They won't let her rest or move. And neither Leslie nor I ask what the dreams are because we feel as if we are dreaming with her. And we all feel it—the impending infiltration—a reign of vitriol, contempt, bigotry, humiliation and mockery, an absence of strategy or plan, anarchy, ignorance, mass shootings and terrorist attacks, resignations, investigations, outcries, breakdowns of systems, and world upheaval on a scale not seen in the twenty-first century. We feel this the same way animals feel an impending earthquake long before it happens.

By May of 2016, a month before the Democratic primary, Leslie is thin, haggard, and desperate; I feel as if every now-sinewy muscle in my body has been stretched and flogged; and Lily looks petrified—literally. Her skin has a hard, bluish-grey tint like stone. Her wispy hair has thinned to the point that, were she anybody else, she would be wearing a wig. She walks bent over, her mouth in a perpetual one-line frown because her lips seem to have retracted out of existence. Out of sheer necessity, she has hired an attendant named Nanette, a forty-five-year-old Black woman who is probably a saint in human guise because she remains steadfastly professional and helpful, no matter how disgruntled and incommunicative Lily is. Even though she's now on Medicare, Lily won't see any doctor except an optometrist for ever-stronger lenses and when I ask, she says the problem is arthritis, although I see no signs of it in her hands or joints. Nanette works three days a week, doing laundry, buying groceries, cooking a week's meals at time, and generally putting up with Lily's silent misanthropy.

At the end of May, the eleventh hour before the Democratic primary, Leslie convinces Lily and me to join her in a phone bank of the three of us in Lily's parlor. "It'll be fun," she says. "I've got a list of numbers of people who have given money, from the campaign office. You can use your flip phone, I'll use my real cell, and Lily can use her landline, and it won't be so scary calling complete strangers if we do it together."

I collapse after two calls, when merely asking if the Bernie Sanders campaign can count on the call recipient's vote elicits first yelling, then crying and a long story about how Hillary Clinton is an evil witch and all is lost.

Leslie makes it through five calls, observed by me and Lily, who hung up on her first call when the line started to ring.

"'If you vant peace, you must make peace,'" says Lily cryptically in a German accent, suddenly looking like an old Jew. Leslie and I give her a look.

"Come again?" I ask.

"Mrs. Schultz," says Lily, as if this explains everything. And for us, it does. We remember how it was because Mrs. S told Lily that to find peace, she had to make peace, and she should do it with other people, and hence, the original Spectators' Club.

It makes sense to the three of us that since we hate talking to people, it might be better to hold a kind of peace vigil. Even if it changes nothing, it might relieve our own tension. And you never know—maybe we will become so peaceful that it will affect people we meet and make them vote for a Democrat, come the election.

"Bullshit," says Leslie.

"Gesundheit," answer Lily and I, and Lily turns off the lights and we sit in a quasi-circle around Mrs. S's much-polished, deeply-scarred nineteenth-century oval mahogany coffee table where the Ouija board once told us to enjoy the exotic zoo that now feels like a roiling inferno where the animals are being burned alive.

After about a minute, our peaceful fug is interrupted by a sequence of piercing tenor barks. "The homosexuals in 3A having sex," says Lily without opening her eyes.

"Must be good to hear it two flights down," I answer.

We all think about sex without opening our eyes. One of the dogs barks in response to the noise, then the other, and we open our eyes and give up on peace.

That night, Lily has a dream: She is a naked little ball-shaped person suddenly bombarded by a blitzkrieg of bullets. They come at her from every direction. Curling into an even tighter ball, her knees to her chin, she tries to become invisible, squeezed into a corner of a soft-walled closet. But she's hit anyway and finds herself floating, falling backwards, down and down, finally coming to a stop in a dark-red cave whose walls and mouth are pulsating and murmuring. Just when she thinks she's safe and can unball herself, a tidal wave erupts through the mouth of the cave, flooding the place, and then the cave walls spasm and bitter fluid fills her mouth and ears, stings her eyes, and burns her skin, but still she hangs onto her cave wall, digging her nails into the red. She holds on so tight that when a giant blue hand reaches into the cave, its long rubbery tentacle fingers feeling around for her, she easily flattens herself out of its detection until the fingers give up and retract out the cave mouth.

Exhausted, naked ball-Lily bunkers, vibrating and pulsating with terror.

Lily never tells me about this dream, but remarkably, I know—because I and then Leslie have the same one. Because we, too, were unplanned pregnancy "mistakes."

None of us are surprised when Hillary Clinton wins the Democratic primary. (We will later learn that it was rigged, but the bias was legal. And none of us will be surprised by that either.)

As the public assumes Clinton's eventual sure-thing victory, Lily, Leslie, and I grip tighter and tighter. Leslie and I grip each other; Lily grips herself—so tight there is no room to touch her. "There is no purpose," she says, when we ask if this is something more than politics.

Gradually we stop checking in with each other in the hope that not saying anything will somehow waylay devastation in November. "Let us be wrong," we pray privately. "Let Lily be wrong."

When we are not wrong, I feel exhausted and battered. Leslie is angry but determined to do whatever it takes to preserve our democracy. And Lily slowly, steadily congeals around her impotence. She turns hard and bitter. She turns into a haughty old stone woman, barely speaking except to give orders to Nanette. And after a while, I stop calling her.

CHAPTER 28

The famous Radio City Music Hall Rockettes are in rebellion. Several have dug in their tap shoe heels and refused to do kick lines at the inauguration celebration for the forty-fifth President of our barely United States, who recently bragged about "grabbing women's pussies" and just sent a celebratory New Years' tweet, addressing his "many enemies who he beat so badly they don't know what to do about it." And a few days ago, a hate group, emboldened by his election, picketed the renowned Juilliard performing arts school a few blocks from us in Lincoln Center. To the tune of "The Battle Hymn of the Republic" they badly sang how God hates Jews. In response, the Juilliard students accompanied them melodically on violins and trumpets, and as the protestors gave up and went away, the two violins broke into *Bach's Concerto for Two Violins* and the onlookers applauded. And in response to all of this, I woke this morning with a throbbing psoas muscle, whose tendency to develop nightly adhesions I'm convinced (due to my brief study of anatomy—a whole other story) is the bane of the aging process.

After a couple of cups of coffee and a quick dog walk, I do my twenty-year-old video Kathy Smith "Winning Workout," practicing extra-creative cursing at Kathy for remaining young with a tight jawline, flat abs, and a well-hydrated psoas as I've aged and must now creak and stretch and consciously lubricate my critical dry transverse muscles into motion. I swear at the new DVR player whose remote signal seems to have hijacked the turn-off signal from the regular TV remote control—it's probably something about the sequence of signals, but I'm too fed up to try to figure it out, so I shut it down manually and, by the time I hit the shower, I'm myself.

I've invited Leslie and Lily to venture out of our neighborhood and meet me for lunch at the Renaissance Restaurant on Ninth Avenue between Fifty-first and Fifty-second Street. It's low key and they have a big back room with a skylight and a brick fireplace where they let you sit as long as you want. I want to sit a long time. I need to see my friends. Leslie is fine, preoccupied by protest marches, and Lily is probably fine, just going through one of her isolation phases. But I'm not fine. I need friends who are smarter than I am, because honestly, I do not know what I'm doing here. I don't know why we do the things we do. I'm absolutely clueless.

However, last night I saw a play. I'm subscribed to a papering service—an organization that supplies audience members to shows that are struggling. For four dollars and fifty cents, I witnessed something numinous, and for the life of me, I don't understand why half the theater was empty. I need to talk to somebody who can hear me, so I called Lily and Leslie late last night, and miraculously, they both said yes to lunch.

The Renaissance Restaurant is not crowded. I'm the first to get there and I stake out a table in the big room and peruse the menu even though I have no interest in food. There are only a couple of other diners and I try to eavesdrop but even in this brick room with a stone floor they are too quiet. I wish it were evening so management would light the fire in the big central fireplace, and I'm thinking of asking when Lily rolls in, pushed in a wheelchair by Nanette. I try not to show my shock.

"Hi. Look at you," I say, getting up.

"Stay where you are," orders Nanette and she expertly removes a chair and rolls Lily up to the table. "I got some errands. How long you think you be?"

Lily shrugs.

"Say an hour and a half?" I ask. And that's when Leslie hustles in.

"Am I late? Sorry. The damned subway. Good god, Lily, are you crippled?"

"I'll be back at one thirty," says Nanette, enunciating as if Lily is deaf. "If it's earlier, call my cell. You got the number in your pocket." And she leaves.

"Are you deaf, Lily?" I ask.

"No, just tired," says Lily, almost cracking a smile. "Exhausted from dreaming." She looks like she's lost her lips in the mass of creases and crevasses that comprise her once beautiful face. Her neck resembles a loose sock. Her once-chiseled Aryan nose seems to have given in to gravity and become elongated, and even through her thick lenses, her eyes have a soft atemporal sheen. "I'm not crippled either. People get out of my way if I use the chair. What's your big news?"

Leslie and I ignore the question, peruse the menu, and then the three of us order. And after the waiter has left, we sit in silence.

"Well," I say after I feel us all settled. "I saw an amazing play last night."

"So you said," says Leslie, and Lily shoots her a "shut up" look.

"It has to do with time. And going to the beginning."

"Of time?" asks Leslie.

"I'm not sure," I say softly, aware that even though I was unable to hear the other diners, they may somehow hear me. "It was a one-man play called *The Encounter*, a true story about how a British writer and explorer, Loren McIntyre, meets the Mayoruna people in the Amazon. The chief of the tribe, who is called Barnacle, talks to McIntyre telepathically—in 'The First Language.'"

We're quiet and we all know what we're thinking—because this is our language.

"The Mayoruna are getting killed by the incursion of civilization, so Barnacle is leading them to return to the beginning. Time is a very fluid thing—not linear. . . I just thought it seemed true."

Lily sips her water. Leslie fingers her silverware. I blow my nose.

"I don't exactly understand where or when the beginning is, but it turns out the only one in the whole tribe who actually knows what they're trying to do is Barnacle. Everybody else is either ignoring him, following him, or fighting him. And in the end, they all disappear. And it seems to me that, through it all, Barnacle was lonely."

Leslie fingers the bread basket even though I know damned well she isn't going to eat the stuff, and gratefully the waiter intercedes with our lunch.

We eat for a while in silence, but I sense that it is time-filling eating rather than hunger or enjoyment of our diner food, which I can't even remember as I write this. In my memory, the food disappears, but we remain.

You may notice that I write this in the present tense, as I write much of this book, because when it is, it *is*. And in truth, it stays *is*. It never becomes was. It is the mind's illusion that it *was*—an illusion due to perspective. All the *is-ing* is contained somehow—by memory? By me writing it? By a greater mind writing it through me? And in that contained state, I wonder: does what happens in one so-called time slice affect the others? I don't know. These are the things I would like to discuss with the other Spectators, but the minute you pull them out of the First Language and put them into words, you lose the context of the so-called First State; the meaning gets distorted and complicated. The thing is, even though I have trouble expressing this, I don't think Lily is confused about what I'm asking when I plead with her to explain what is going on. If Lily understands more than I do, and if she would share it, maybe we all could share it, and we'd stop being so lonely and upset as we await Trump-ageddon. And while we wait, maybe we'll have some sense of purpose. Which at the moment, I'm devoid of.

"You see," I continue when it is clear that nobody else is going to speak. "You see, Barnacle is the only one who knew. Maybe that's the way it is, I don't know. Maybe even though Barnacle knew and managed to tell it to Loren McIntyre, Loren McIntyre couldn't truly understand—or, in the First Language, know—until he told the story. It's as if he was supposed to understand, to *know* firsthand the truth, when he later tells the story of what happens with Barnacle. So others might *know*. And then he'd have company. Does any of this sound familiar?"

Lily picks at her front teeth with the tip of one of her cracked fingernails. "It drives me crazy that food gets stuck. This is a part of getting old that I absolutely abhor. Does anyone have some floss? Or a toothpick?"

Leslie digs in her purse and supplies a little white box of floss.

Lily discretely frees the piece of whatever it was that she ate.

The other two diners signal the waiter for their check, pay, and leave quickly.

None of us are nonplussed.

"Threads. So skinny yet so strong," says Lily contemplatively, balling up the floss and hiding it under the edge of her plate. "You know, I used to have a belly button phobia."

Leslie and I are afraid to look at each other or breathe.

"I couldn't touch it—or anybody else's. I was born that way. But suddenly, this morning, miraculously without thinking, I saw a speck of dirt in my belly button and pulled it out. I've been back to the beginning. I simply stared at the problem until the connections revealed themselves and therefore the breaks could be found and mended. Isn't that amazing?"

There is something Lily understands that just won't gel for me, and I'm sure Leslie doesn't completely get it either. I try again.

"That's amazing, Lily. I am very happy for you. Maybe you suddenly saw it differently. You know, at the beginning of the play that I went to, the actor/writer Simon McBurney is in his apartment in London. Everybody in the audience wears headphones and the voices of his little girl and all kinds of sound effects come through and they seem to come from all different directions—off to the sides of the theater, behind us, above. You believe his little girl is speaking just behind your left ear. Then when the story shifts to the Amazon jungle and McBurney plays Loren McIntyre with all the jungle sounds, I don't know how to communicate it, but you're *there* and McBurney is McIntyre. You actually forget you're sitting in the first balcony of a Broadway theater watching an actor with high-tech microphones; your context shifts and you're *in* the jungle. You smell it and sweat! You see it differently. These transformations are real."

"Sounds wonderful," says Lily, again cracking that odd lipless smile, which makes me shudder for reasons I don't understand.

"The point being that reality, like time, is malleable. It's all about *how* we are perceiving. It's not fixed. How I'm perceiving right now is that a small portion of our country overturned the wishes of the majority and elected an Emperor with No Clothes, a Mad Hatter, a nut case with nuclear bomb codes, and my muscles are jamming up on me and when I woke this morning, I was so sore, I couldn't bend over to reach the milk on the lower shelf in my refrigerator."

"And what are we supposed to do about it?" snaps Lily. "It's the sequence. It's just the sequence. I don't understand it any more than you do. Just what the hell do you want from me? I am not a goddamned container!"

This is not what I expected. Neither did Leslie; I can tell by the way she flushes.

"It's just that you're a psychic," I try, but Lily flips off my comment with a haughty queen's gesture.

I persist: "Sometimes I dream about you, Lily." I don't know why I'm telling her this, but I go with the impulse. "Sometimes I think you're dreaming about me at the same time. And Leslie. It's like we're meeting in a dream form. But I don't know what we're doing. And when I wake up, I can't remember more than the meeting."

Lily's face is becoming so constricted and red, if I didn't know better I would think she was having a bowel movement.

"Are you all right, Lily? I just—. If you'd just explain. If you'd tell us what is going on."

"The whole world has a belly button phobia!" she announces, shoving herself away from the table with such force that she rolls into the table behind her. "Lacuna calls. I have to go."

"To the bathroom?" asks Leslie who is similarly interpreting her facial expression.

"For god's sake, no! Nanette!" she yells into the air.

"Lily, take it easy. I didn't mean to upset you. I just thought—"

Plunging her hand into her pocket, she pulls out wads of Kleenex, a couple of quarters, and a piece of paper which she throws on the table. "Goddammit! I need the other glasses!" she says, ripping off the ones on her face and throwing them onto our table as she searches for reading lenses in her other pocket.

"Easy, Lily, easy," I say, snatching the piece of paper. "I'll call her."

And I dial Nanette, who it turns out is rushing into the restaurant that very moment. Does she have a psychic umbilical cord to Lily as well? As Lily tosses about her wheelchair, Nanette bustles into our big room, takes over, neatens Lily's jacket, orders her to calm herself, and miraculously, Lily sinks into the chair, instantly looking shrunken, bows her head once—"good-bye"—and mumbles something that sounds like "It's in your hands, Betsy. Check under the floorboard." And they're gone.

Silence.

"What the fuck?" says Leslie.

"I don't know. I don't know."

To recover, we both order tea. When it comes, we look at it until Leslie suddenly notices Lily's glasses hidden under our napkins and her old Kleenexes when she threw them onto the table. "I've had enough for one day," she says, handing them to me.

"Don't worry. I'll do it."

I pocket the glasses. We pay, splitting Lily's tab and leaving our tea undrunk.

Leslie has an appointment downtown and I hop on a Tenth Avenue uptown bus.

The ride uptown is blessedly slow and calm in the half-empty bus. I gaze out the window seeing nothing, feeling nothing, in a kind of after-a-heavy-social-scene trance until I am roused by loud static on the driver's radio.

"Sorry, folks," he yells, making a sharp left off-route at Fifty-seventh Street. "We're being detoured. Express stops only on West End Ave. Next stop, Seventy-second."

Fine. Just two blocks from my normal stop. I'll go by Lily's place on West Seventy-fourth and return the eyeglasses.

There is nothing to look at on West End which is fine. It's a blur as we speed north, making an abrupt stop at the corner of Seventy-second Street. Even from there—one long block from Broadway to the east—I can hear the sirens. Is there a fire at the subway stop? It looks like it. A bad one. Maybe if I walk on the north side of Seventy-second I can by-pass it and still take the quickest route to Lily's.

I hoof it, speed walking to get past the mess, zipping around people on the crowded sidewalk outside of Kinkos. Everybody loves an accident. In no time, I've wormed my way to the corner of Broadway opposite the new subway depot and Verdi Square. The fire appears to be in front of the old depot on the south side of the street. A van is on fire and the smoke is so thick it's hard to breathe. This was a stupid idea. So what if I have to walk an extra block or so. I'll turn north and then—

But the crowd has another idea and before I can make a decision I'm being herded across the street, and that's when I see Lily, alone in her chair behind a couple of teenage girls who are squealing and gawking. Where the hell's Nanette? "Lily!" I holler, but she doesn't seem to see me.

There's too much noise, too many people, fire fighters, cops everywhere. There's one coming toward the girls who looks like a member of some kind of elite SWAT team, dressed head to toe in navy blue with a big NYPD patch on his arm and a scary looking rifle. He's probably going to clear the area. This is not an ordinary accident.

"Lily!" I yell as loud as I can, but the cop is herding them all—the girls, Lily, other onlookers—north, waving his rifle for them to move. What the hell is going on? "Lily!" I yell.

And just then the cop freezes, takes a stance, lifts his rifle. *Pop-pop-pop-pop*!

I dive. People scatter. Bullets fly. Screams, cries. It only takes seconds and somebody, another cop, takes him down.

"Hands up everybody!" he orders. "Hands up! Now!"

I can't move. I'm on the ground in the middle of Broadway on top of several people. Lily's crushed glasses are cutting into my hand, but otherwise, no blood. But I can't move. I'm shaking too hard. People around me push me off, climb to their feet. Somebody grabs me by the back of my coat, hauls me to my feet, yanks my arms into the air, and disappears.

"Hands up!" booms the cop. "If you're injured or next to somebody who is, yell."

There is all kinds of yelling, but I'm not hurt, and I stand there with my hands waving, gasping through the singed acrid air, shaking so hard I feel like my skeleton is coming apart. Lily. Where's Lily? I look to the spot where she was and her chair is empty. People. People everywhere. On the ground. Everywhere. "Lily!" I yell into the killing field.

The cop—the shooter who got the man with the rifle—is moving toward a pile that has become a heaving human mountain. "Are you all right?" I hear him yell.

A brown-haired girl is hysterical. Her back is covered with blood as she pushes what looks like a dead body off her and struggles to her feet. Then a girl in yellow parka, equally bloody, shoves her way out from under the body and, with steely-jawed determination, points her cell phone at the cop and continues filming.

"Medics!" yells the cop, and suddenly two of them are on the spot, turning the brown-haired girl around, examining her back.

"It's not me!" she shrieks. "It's the old lady. She jumped on top of us."
And that's when I see it is Lily.

CHAPTER 29

One perfect *pop* to the head. That's all it took to take the shooter down. When I clean out Lily's stuff, I find the diaries detailing every thought and permutation going back to high school. I learn that in the last few months she has been traveling at night, seeing things in Dreamland, helping people, getting to know the girl in the yellow parka. She has been acting as a servant of so-called time, seeing the whole thread, back to her conception and beyond, and thereby mending her blind spots, seeing the necessity that all systems break down in order for renaissance— rebirth. But in awake life, she was just like Barnacle. Alone, anonymous, held in no particular esteem by anyone who visited her for psychic counseling or who sold her groceries in the local shops or checked out her library books. One context blots out another.

Lily was no leader or chief. For thirty seconds on the six o'clock news, she was the selfless elderly lady who leapt onto the girls, only to be forgotten by the time she was identified because the news cycle had moved on.

Lily was assiduous about thoughts and events in her diaries, but in the hundreds of thousands of entries I read, nowhere were there feelings; the First Language is untranslatable; the First Language is *knowing* infused with feeling that informed her every action and inability to act. So of course I cannot know what really happened, why she did what she did. But here is what I believe:

There is a crazy whirlpool energy just before the van crashes. And when it comes—the explosion—is it an accident? Nanette, who has medical training, parks Lily out of harm's way and runs to assist. Without her glasses, Lily has only her other senses to rely on and on opening them, she is nearly electrocuted by static energy. Like a lightning umbilical cord, it pierces, time stops, contexts merge, and she surrenders to the strange waves and buzzing that rip through the atmosphere, sending the Verdi Square pigeons careening through space, zigging, zagging, their flock scattered like fury. And in a reverse reaction, Lily, who normally cannot see anything, sees everything. Sans eyeglasses, she simply stares at the problem until the connections reveal themselves and therefore the breaks can be found and mended. To a bystander, she might appear to be daydreaming, but in truth, she has undergone another kind of infiltration—inundated in her Self, her vision of here and now, in all contexts, is pristine, clear, as if from the point of view of somebody sitting inside everything, and anywhere she focuses, there is beauty. And with the beauty is the ever-expanding chasm of pain in her heart at not having been connected to it before. Or not having *known* she was connected. And with connection comes the pain of loss of connection. And with that comes the full pain of the rejection by her mother and all the grief she never felt at the deaths of her parents and brothers and even her sister. She feels each death like a blow to her heart, leaving it wider, deeper. It's as if the static clears her and simultaneously ejects her into nonspace-nontime-all-contexts, from which she can view all the so-called time slices, all the kaleidoscopic boxes, with perfect vision. And from this place, she surrenders her need to control or even understand the sequences, and in that letting go she sees or remembers the endings of all of her friends and acquaintances—me, Harmony, Leslie, Zelda, Lucresse, Mrs. S who really did know her, Philip, Martin, the Shoren brothers, the Scully sisters, Kiana, all the miserable Madoffs, and the unnamed but deeply loved fetus. She remembers all the unknown ancestors: The pogrom-fleeing Jews, one of whom landed in Oklahoma at the beginning of the American oil industry and, to steal headrights ownership of minerals, married an Osage Indian who wove a Crow blanket; the Russian and Polish peasants who did not survive; the exiled tribes of Israel; the gatherers who broke off from the hunters tens of thousands of so-called years ago and, ignoring the herd and without strong impulses to procreate, studied plants, following the lifeline back to seed, whereupon they domesticated them, providing sustenance for the ever-ballooning populations. Then back even further to the divergent genetic lineage of the Haplogroup T clan that bore the agriculturalists, and back and back to the mother of us all in East Africa, Mitochondrial Eve. And even further still, she remembers the helpers: the voice who told her to hang on tight to her flying saucer sled as it was flown over the tree stump; the unnamed ones who listened with her to Bach that very first time so that she would know that bliss existed, the family of invisible Spectators who have always been there watching, applauding, and cheering her on. And back even further she goes to the All That Is, the Great Compassion and Intelligence, to the Creator that was so lonely for company that it created the stories. And seeing that, Lily remembers endings that have happened and those that have yet to be. And in memory, she sees the perfection—expansion and contraction—and how we are who we are because it is right. We have the life we have because we are part of something much bigger than we can imagine, something that is ever changing through love and destruction, and the part we each play requires the life we have in a community—a herd—that is and will always be. It has nothing to do with being worthy or unworthy. It simply *is*. One's life *is*. And with that thought, she dives— not to escape, but to save—because she cares! She cares, she loves, she can admit it finally, and she saves the girl in the yellow parka—another spectator who cannot move. She saves her, knowing that for the stories to exist, there must be spectators, but in this story, she is finally an actor.

And with that knowing, Lily, like her beloved Stoner, knows she is good and whole, has always been so, and has never been alone. It comes upon her with a sudden force, and she feels its power. She is herself, a spectator *and* an actor, and that is exactly what she was meant to be.

EPILOGUE

Remember Barnacle? How he knew what was coming and somehow managed to telepathize it to Loren McIntyre, but Loren McIntyre couldn't truly understand—or, in the First Language, *know*—until he told the story in a book? It's as if he was supposed to understand, to *know* firsthand the truth, when he later tells the story of what happens with Barnacle. So others might *know*. And then he'd have company.

Remember "Lacuna calls," that weird thing Lily said at our last lunch? I looked it up. Lacuna is an unfilled space, a gap, a missing part, and I think that's where it—everything—really lives: us, stories, knowing, and who knows what. And to us it appears as missing, but some people know better.

I'm no Barnacle or Lily. But like Lily, I've never truly known my purpose. However, as I've gone through her things, read her diaries and used them to tell this story, I've come to believe that for some people—perhaps the spectators of the world—purpose and the sequence of our birth and lives are none of our business. Thinking we know is just another illusion, a distraction from the mandate to live, be kind, and do our best to see the story everybody else is so briefly and busily performing in the tiny box of time slices that comprise our context—because it is so darned interesting! And awe-inspiring.

Lily could seem like an airhead, but you don't become independently wealthy by being stupid. She left an airtight will—bequeathing to her estranged husband, Philip, who of course came sniffing after he learned about her on the news, only the "Birthday" print and naming me as executrix.

As I clean and organize and donate and dispose, I play Lily's many recordings of *Bach's Concerto for Two Violins and Orchestra in D minor* and, although I never experience the bliss Lily chased all her life, I find it soothing, comforting. I play it on the house speakers—it turns out Lily knew a thing or two about wiring, so I can even hear it in her bedroom, the last room I tackle. And when the music finally stops, I notice there is an almost imperceptible hum. A pulse. A heat whose source I cannot pinpoint. And I like it.

This is the only room that really looks like Lily. No antique furniture. Just a plain pine Ikea bed, a small throw rug, a few dog toys, Lucresse's painting of three women sitting around a table laughing, and an oddly blanketed closet mirror. I throw out most of the stuff, pack the painting for myself—on its back, in Lily's neat block printing: "A great shift is coming." What on earth could that mean? I fold the ratty crow-faced mirror blanket for what I don't know—maybe it's an antique. Then I start disassembling the bed which will never fit through the doorway intact. And as I'm piling the neatly marked pieces—did Lily do this purposefully, knowing that someday the bed would be taken apart by somebody like me with no mechanical talent?—I see the loose floorboard. It is sticking up at an angle so you can't miss it. I don't want to go into great detail, but suffice it say that Lily was a very good friend and I no longer worry about finding editing gigs.

Like Lily, I'm doing my best to watch. I watch from a bird's eye view, just this side of Lacuna, when I can lift out of my ego, which is not that often. It is hard to avoid our herd's proclivity for misery porn—an exaggeration, an addiction, a distraction like any other—and still stay informed. Leslie and I moan only to one another about the latest events in the fast-moving devastation known as the forty-fifth President of the United States, and, in an effort to become spectators who also act, we have become demonstration buddies—marching, carrying signs, and relentlessly calling our representatives to express our outrage, while abstaining from adding to the heat with social media venting. The shootings are escalating. Most recently—on February 14, Lily's sixty-seventh birthday—in Parkland, Florida, which is how I learn about a girl from New York:

Six months after the now-famous terrorist attack at the Seventy-second Street subway, a girl named Cathy relocated to Broward County, Florida—moved by her parents to escape big-city violence. Their hope was that Cathy, who had taken an interest in journalism, would thrive in the nationally renowned program offered at the Marjory Stoneman

Douglas High School.

She is alive.

Relief.

That sounds odd, I know. But that's what you feel when you see—from that bird's eye view—that the story is inevitable, not yours to control, and love is pure; unattached to outcome, it acts. You stop fighting. You give in. Your revere everything. You participate. And you share it. You share it to know it. And it's as if you've known the object of your affection—life— long before you could see it. You look; you see with old eyes; and you say, as if it's for the first time, although it's been forever: "I'm so relieved I'm here. I'm so glad I'm me. In this story, wherever it leads."

ABOUT THE AUTHOR

Betsy Robinson writes funny fiction about flawed people. Her novel *The Last Will & Testament of Zelda McFigg* is winner of Black Lawrence Press's 2013 Big Moose Prize and was published in September 2014. This was followed by the February 2015 publication of her edit of *The Trouble with the Truth* by Edna Robinson, Betsy's late mother, by Simon & Schuster/Infinite Words. She published revised e-book and paperback editions of her Mid-List Press award-winning first novel, a tragicomedy about falling down the rabbit hole of the U.S. of A. in the 1970s, *Plan Z by Leslie Kove*, when it went out of print. Her articles have been published in *Publishers Weekly*, Lithub, *Oh Reader*, The Sunlight Press, *Prairie Fire*, Journal of Compressed Creative Arts, Salvation South, Next Avenue, and many other publications. Betsy is an editor, fiction writer, journalist, playwright, and former actor. Her website is www.BetsyRobinson-writer.com.

ACKNOWLEDGMENTS

I wrote *The Spectators* over the course of years, pausing for a couple to find out what would happen politically. I had no sense of whether anybody else would read it. It felt like a life and book wrap-up, a ritual that intrigued and, as it was born, informed me. I didn't know when I began that protagonists from my other books, let alone a character version of me, would become part of the story. But they did. Therefore I would like to acknowledge their original births from writer's ether:

Leslie Kove first made my acquaintance in *Plan Z by Leslie Kove*, published by Mid-List Press in 2001 as winner of their First Novel Award Series and later revised into a second edition when the paperback went out of print. Thank you to Marianne Nora and Lane Stiles of Mid-List.

Although Zelda McFigg was the third protagonist to take birth—in *The Last Will & Testament of Zelda McFigg* published by Black Lawrence Press in 2014 as winner of their Big Moose Prize (thank you to Diane Goettel and the crew of Black Lawrence), she was preceded by Harmony Rogers in *Cats on a Pole*, published by Kano Press in 2024.

Lucresse Briard in reality was born to my late mother, Edna Robinson, when she first drafted her novel *The Trouble with the Truth* in 1959, which was then edited by me and published by Simon & Schuster/Atria/Infinite Words in 2015. Thank you to Charmaine Roberts Parker and Zane at Infinite Words.

I am indebted to Edna not only for Lucresse's and my own birth, but for Lily's mother's monologue detailing the visit to her father and the train trip home to Oklahoma. This was part of an unpublished article that Edna wrote, and since she left all her writing to me, I have used a revised excerpt, not only because I love the writing, but to include her in this wrap-up. (I am merging contexts, if you will.)

I would like to thank my intrepid literary agent, Sara Camilli, for finding a home for my mother's novel.

Thanks to my friend Alicia Ogawa for our book-talk walks and for the rich experiences that she has generously exposed me to that I have blatantly stolen for this book.

Thank you to my long-time colleague, brilliant, elegant designer, John Goryl, and inspired cover artist, Susan A. Pascale, a violin player who creates art like music.

Thank you to Petru Popescue for his book *The Encounter: Amazon Beaming* and to Simon McBurney for his theatrical translation of it in his remarkable Broadway production.

Thank you to David James Duncan whose book *Sun House* broke open my heart and blew off the top of my head, inspiring me to contact him from across the vast Ocean to ask him to blurb this book. In an unfathomable act of generosity, he said he would read the book (unheard of in publishing, where most blurbers read a few pages and a synopsis) but would make no promises . . . only to respond with every writer's fantasy of reader understanding and enthusiasm.

Because I want to tell as much of the whole untranslatable "knowing truth" as is possible, I would like to thank photographer and humanitarian Gordon Parks. I never met the man but in 1996 when I was a freelance transcriptionist, the agency I was working for gave me a series of taped interviews done by photographer John Loengard of the original *LIFE* magazine photographers, and I was lucky enough to receive Gordon Parks, whose words and energy I've never forgotten. Recently I reread my proofing copy of the transcript and was once again overwhelmed by his compassion and energy. Shortly after this, a propos of nothing, I thought of blurbers for this book, and I heard Mr. Parks's deep, kind voice say, as he did so many times in his interview, "Why not try?" And it was because of that that I reached out to David James Duncan.

And it was because of a conversation with brilliant, beautiful sociologist and polymath Bertice Berry, PhD, at one of her retreats in Boone, NC, that I reread the Gordon Parks transcript, ended up writing an article about it for *Next Avenue*, and was open to Mr. Parks's help. And it was also because of Bertice—an exercise she led at another retreat in Boone—that I started Kano Press. Thank you, Bertice, for being a conduit of love and inspiration to me as well as all who are lucky enough to be with you.

I would like to add a belated thank you, that really belonged in *Cats on a Pole*, to the late Levent Bolukbasi and his IM School of Healing Arts. One of the most powerful exercises we did in this school was falling backwards off a table into the knitted arms of fellow classmates. I had no problem falling or "surrendering," but I'd gotten into trouble by doing it in a certain oblivion—I didn't understand how one could simultaneously surrender and control. Just before this class another student explained to me that her understanding of surrender is that one does it with awareness. The day of the falling exercise, I watched her demonstrate this, and I could not get up on that table fast enough, because finally I understood the thing that had eluded me all my life. And I did it: I looked in the eyes of all the catchers, connected, turned my back, asked if everybody was ready. "Yes," they answered with all the solemnity I felt. And I fell.

Writing a book is like falling backwards, and for me the "flukiest" part of that is eleventh-hour revisions: I'll be reading something else, see a word, and suddenly realize that word belongs in the book I'm finalizing. Or an impulse seems to come out of nowhere, spurring a revision I'd never considered. If I understand that this "stuff" does not come out of "nowhere," that there is no fluke, then I am surrendering with awareness to so-called Lacuna and there is no fear or helplessness. There is gratitude and humility.

We live in a multiverse of contexts. Everything and everyone is connected. Nobody dies.

And with that understanding, I would like to thank the late John Williams for writing *Stoner*, a perfect book that says everything there is to say about life, thereby changing mine.

PICTURE CREDITS

"Frederick Law Olmstead" by John Singer Sargent. This is a faithful photographic reproduction of a two-dimensional, public domain work of art. The work of art itself is in the public domain for the following reason:
https://commons.wikimedia.org/wiki/File:Frederick_Law_Olmsted.jpg The author died in 1925, so this work is in the public domain in its country of origin and other countries and areas where the copyright term is the author's life plus 80 years or less.

Robert Burns statue. Photo by Betsy Robinson, statue by John Steell, Central Park, NYC.

Walter Scott statue. Photo by Betsy Robinson, statue by John Steell, Central Park, NYC.

Hans Christian Andersen statue. Photo by Betsy Robinson, statue by Georg John Lober, Central Park, NYC.

Alice in Wonderland statue, Photo by Betsy Robinson, statue by José de Creeft, Central Park, NYC. (Dog is my late dog Maya, playing the role of Leslie Kove's dog, Spud. Apologies for the seasonal inappropriateness; there would be no snow in summer.)

TEXT CREDITS

The Art of War by Sun Tzu. NY: Penguin Books, 2009.

The Devil in the White City by Erik Larson. NY: Vintage Books,
a division of Random House, Inc., 2004.

First Encounter by Bella Chagall. NY: Schocken, 1987.

Stoner by John Williams. NY: The New York Review of Books, 2003.

Epigraphs for Parts I, II, and III. "Study finds cells maintain a complete
molecular 'memory' of their embryonic origins" by Dana-Farber Cancer
Institute. Phys.org, March 21, 2019.

ABOUT KANO PRESS

Kano Press takes its name from the oracle rune Kano, which stands for Opening, Fire, Torch. A rune is a letter in a runic alphabet used to write Germanic languages before the Latin alphabet was adopted. The symbol for kano is <, or reversed >. Runes inscribed on small stone pieces that are blindly drawn from a bag are used to aid our understanding of whatever issue we choose or to provide guidance. Drawing < signifies opening and renewed clarity, freedom to both receive gifts and to know the joy of nonattached giving. If one draws the reversed position, >, it signifies a darkening of the light and advises to give up the old, live on empty, develop inner stability, and wait for illumination.

Three guiding quotations:

> "I mean, if you have any idea of any kind of complexity or immensity or destiny, of general order, you're put in a position of nothingness. And I think this is true. I don't think I'm anything; I never have thought that. Whatever it is that activates it is a certain kind of energy that goes on. But the effect is ridiculous; it's absurd."
> —LINCOLN KIRSTEIN in *The New Yorker*

> "When I see heavy dramas with no comic relief, I don't think they're honest. I don't think people go through life miserable all the time; in fact, if you're very miserable, you giggle a lot at the oddest things."
> —CARL REINER in *The Trib*

"In the same way that . . . the listener completes the song, I
believe if you give them a certain sound and you place it just
far enough so that they can just hear it, it creates a depth
in your hearing and that depth, just like if you imagine the
church bells in the distance, there's something about that
that opens the listener . . . there's something about these
distant sounds that open us up emotionally and if as a writer,
a songwriter, I can produce sounds that allow the listener
to open themselves emotionally, then whatever I have to say
lyrically has a chance of being really meaningful."
                          —PAUL SIMON, "Smartless" podcast

Kano Press aspires to publish books that include humor and a
transcendent point of view, stories that evoke openings.

Cats on a Pole
A metaphysical love story of two psychically-gifted people who are isolated—like cats stuck up on a telephone pole—by their gifts.

Plan Z by Leslie Kove
A funny and poignant novel about negotiating life without a plan, without a clue. With PTSD.

Girl Stories & Game Plays
24 stories and 3 one-act plays—a feast of silly, serious, strange, sexy, transcendent, and laugh-out-loud funny stories and plays with playable scenes

The Last Will & Testament of Zelda McFigg
A raucously funny novel about doing whatever is necessary to survive. Winner of Black Lawrence Press's Big Moose Prize

The Trouble with the Truth
An actor's sister's story of growing up in the shadow of her dramatic brother in the 1930s and '40s. (Edited by Betsy, written by her late mother, Edna.)

Conversations with Mom: An Aging Baby Boomer, in Need of an Elder, Writes to Her Dead Mother
A funny and moving little book for anyone who's struggled with being human.

www.ingramcontent.com/pod-product-compliance
Lightning Source LLC
Chambersburg PA
CBHW031025160726
47991CB00005B/1876